To Heather, with my appreciation

A Talisman of Home

Annie M Ballard

Annie M. Ballard

Published by Annie M. Ballard, 2021.

This is a work of fiction. Similarities to real people, places, or events are entirely coincidental.

A TALISMAN OF HOME

First edition. July 4, 2021.

Copyright © 2021 Annie M. Ballard.

ISBN: 978-17777416-0-0

Written by Leslie Ann Costello as Annie M. Ballard.

Published by Devon Station Books, Fredericton, NB, Canada

All rights reserved.

Stella Mare

MACKIE'S EYES BURNED with the strain of trying to see around the dark curves of the twisty road down to the shore. Almost anything could be around the corner in this Canadian wilderness. Murphy, her fuzzy goldendoodle, whined from the back seat, feeling her stress. She wished she'd left earlier, missed the construction, maybe even turned around to go back home. Anything to avoid this nasty feeling that she was driving into nothing.

But she had to go on. She hadn't any home to go back to and, even though she couldn't see around the curve, she hoped that there was something ahead of her.

She slowed to a crawl, but then headlights appeared in her rearview mirror prompting her to accelerate slightly. The oversized pickup behind her sped up and passed her despite the curve.

"Whoa, Murph, did you see that? Guess people here have second sight or something." Murphy huffed in assent.

"Guess I better get on with it though." Mackie's phone gave her the next direction and she felt relief when she landed on the flat and saw a little town ahead. Ah, streetlights!

In the stillness of the very late evening, Mackie drove through the quiet downtown, aware of the water to her right and shops to her left. Her directions took her through town and up a small hill to the left. Finally she heard her phone tell her, "Destination is on your left."

In the moonlight, there wasn't much to see, just a slash of driveway in the shrubs. She pulled in, driving up close to the dark house. "Well, Murph, this is it. Our new home, at least for a while." She fumbled to find the keys and they headed to the porch.

As she struggled to unlock the dead bolt, a wave of excitement built in her belly. Or was it fear? She decided she'd call it excitement and just quiet the scary thoughts for now. Murphy sniffed around the yard, watering where he deemed it appropriate, and then scrambled up on the porch, dancing with excitement as she wrestled with the key. It finally turned with ease and Mackie pushed inward to take her first look inside. Murphy pushed past her and his nails scrabbled on the hardwood of the hall.

Mackie fumbled for light switches and finally illuminated a wide hallway with a wooden staircase. She caught the faint scent of a fireplace filled with last year's ashes, damp but fragrant. It was not unpleasant. Mackie wandered to the kitchen, turning on lights as she went, then through the comfortable living room then up the stairs. When Mackie saw the bed, her fatigue nearly overcame her. She quickly pulled off her jeans and T-shirt, snapped off the light, and headed for the bed. Ignoring most of the bedding piled on the mattress, she tugged a cozy-looking blanket free and wrapped herself up. Falling onto the bed, she could feel fatigue moving through her body.

Tomorrow she must figure out where to find food, company, and especially, the person she was seeking. For tonight, she would sleep. She gratefully settled into the bed.

A RACKET OF BIRDSONG outside the bedroom window woke Mackie the next morning. She groaned and looked at her watch. *Five a.m.! Ugh.* But Murphy was up and clicking around on the hardwood so she unwrapped the blanket and stood up. Her mouth felt full of fur and all she could think of was a shower. First, she needed to see the house in daylight.

Letting Murphy out the front door, she breathed in salt air. What was that smell? Oh, honeysuckle. The luxuriant vines covered the sides of the porch, filling the trellis at the far end with tiny yellow trumpets. Murphy sniffed around the yard. Mackie grabbed her keys and unloaded her stuff from the car. There wasn't much. Her laptop. Her backpack suitcase. A box that contained Murphy's essentials. Her bike was attached to the rack on the back of the ancient Toyota Corolla. It didn't take long to unload the car.

Mackie went back inside to the sunny kitchen with a tiny table, two chairs, and white cabinets. Was there a coffee maker? She located the machine, but no coffee.

"Oh, right," she muttered to herself. "Should have brought coffee. It's five a.m.; there won't be coffee anywhere for a while." She set the kettle to boil and scrounged a dusty tea bag.

Cup in hand, she wandered through the house. The living room had a wood-burning stove and a squishy-looking couch, a worn Persian rug, and shelves and shelves of books. There was also an old stereo system like Mackie remembered from the home of one of her friends' grandparents, but she had no idea how to use it. Behind a cabinet door she found a more modern TV. When Mackie pulled out her phone to check, she saw that the Wi-Fi network showed up. Relief! She needed that in order to work. Quickly, she located the email from Dr. Hamilton with the details about the house and entered the password. Connected. *Small steps,* she told herself. *Keep moving forward.*

Hearing scratching on the door, she let Murphy in. She had no fear of him running off. As long as he knew where she was, he stuck around. "Hey, Murph. Anything interesting out there? No coffee here, but let's go get your breakfast." She settled him with his kibble.

Later she would go to town to find some coffee and groceries. Later. Right now she wanted to settle into this new place and see if it might feel like the refuge she needed. See if it might eventually bring some sense of home. She refilled her mug of tea and sank into the softness of the blue sofa.

What would Sarah think if she could see this? What would she tell Mackie? "Mum would tell me I'm crazy," she said aloud. "She'd say I was trying to find something that doesn't exist and that I should just go back to Somerville. At least I might know somebody there."

Murphy wandered in and jumped up on the sofa next to her. He curled up and tried to get in her lap despite his size. "Oh, Murphy," she murmured. "I think you're the only one I have left." He let out a big sigh and rested his head on her knee, looking up with his deep brown eyes that seemed to see right inside of her. "This is a crazy thing, isn't it, buddy? We're doing something kind of crazy, but maybe it's better to be a little crazy than to die of sadness."

MACKIE'S COFFEE-DEPRIVED body pointed her downtown before seven a.m. She'd taken a shower in the old-fashioned claw-foot tub with a handheld sprayer, pulled on clean clothes and sneakers, and threw her laptop into the car. The main street was still quiet, but the day was bright, even this early, and several trucks were parked along one part of the street. "Yup," Mackie said to herself, "breakfast and coffee, right there."

Carrying her laptop bag, she hesitantly leaned against the glass and ancient oak door of the Sunshine Diner and slid inside. As she looked for an empty table, she was aware of a sudden quiet in the restaurant. Then the talk and laughter resumed. She headed straight for a small booth toward the back, but in sight of the door and the loud group of men in working clothes and ball caps seated at the counter and at tables near the front.

The server waved at her from the end of the counter. "Hey, there," she called, giving Mackie a big grin. "Coffee? Latte?"

"Oh, please, coffee." Mackie nodded with gratitude. Sleep was great, but three hours were just not enough. Coffee might help.

"Hi," said the young woman in a black tank and jeans when she arrived at the table. "I'm Cassandra." She poured steaming coffee into the large pottery mug in front of Mackie. Mackie peeked up at her face. She had a mop of inky hair tied into a curly bundle, jewelry adorning nostrils, earlobes, and lip, and a stunning multicolored tattoo sleeve on her pouring arm.

Mackie couldn't help herself. "Wow! That's amazing art on your arm." She peered at the tattoo.

Cassandra grinned, set down the coffeepot, and held her arm so Mackie could look more closely. "Yeah, it's pretty cool, isn't it? I did some of the design myself. It's nice to hear someone appreciate it."

Mackie looked up at her. "You designed it yourself? Do you do this sort of art regularly?"

Cassandra shook her head. "No, not really. I just had an idea and went with it. Here's a menu, but I really recommend the cinnamon rolls." She raised her striking eyebrows. "My uncle makes them and they are the best ever. Way better than those airport ones."

Mackie was a little lost…airport ones? Oh, yes, the chain of cinnamon roll stores. "Okay, thanks for the suggestion. I'll have one, thanks, Cassandra," she tried out the name.

"Yep, that's me," the girl said. "And you're not from here, are you?"

Mackie looked down. Small towns meant people were known or not known. She had tried to prepare for this.

"Right. I'm not. My name is Ken…Mack. Mackie." Cassandra's expressive brows asked a question. "Yeah, my name is Mackenzie and I go by Mackie. But I used to be called something else. I'm Mackie. I'm visiting for a while."

"Okay, then, hello, Mackie. You can be sure everyone's going to want to know all about the new girl. I'll go get your food and check in later."

As she walked off, Mackie felt both relief and a little sadness. She sipped her coffee (blessed brew) and pulled out her laptop. The diner had Wi-Fi enough that she might do a little work or at least check in on some projects while she was here. This trip might be a shot in the dark, but she had to keep up her work while here.

Mackie sensed something and looked up to see Cassandra sashaying toward the front of the restaurant where the group of working men were finishing breakfast. Cassandra thumbed back toward her and said something. A few men at the counter looked her way briefly, but then headed for the cash register.

One man looked a little longer. He caught Mackie's eye and lifted a hand in a brief salute. She looked quickly down at her laptop, as if she didn't see. Immediately she berated herself. *Why are you so ridiculous? How are you going to find what you need to find if you are too scared to talk to anybody?*

Geez Louise, Mack, you need a confidence transplant.

OVER THE NEXT HOUR, the diner cleared out except for a few older patrons and Mackie plus her laptop. Cassandra dropped by her table.

"Is it okay for me to stick around here and do some work as long as I keep drinking coffee?" Mackie asked.

Cassandra grinned. "Heck, yeah. We are certainly not overrun with tourists yet. And the guys won't be back in until late. They're all out on the water by now."

"On the water?"

"Yeah, a lot of them work on the water. So where are you from?"

Mackie swallowed hard. "Are you off work now? You can sit down if it's okay with your boss."

"Oh, sure, Sonny doesn't care. As long as everyone gets their coffee, it's okay." Cassandra dusted the seat with her towel and sat down, elbows on the table, chin in her hands. "So tell me all about you."

Mackie leaned as far back as she could. This stuff was hard. But she had a plan. Tell enough, but not too much. Get connected, but keep your own counsel. Do not get attached. Do not get attached. Do not get attached.

"Yeah, so I am house-sitting for the Hamiltons while they're off to wherever. On a mission trip or something like that. Somebody in my town is a cousin of theirs, so anyway, that's how I heard about it."

"Where's your town? You don't sound like a local really," Cassandra commented.

"You're right, I'm not. I'm from Massachusetts, actually, north of Boston." This much was true.

"Ha! You're an American!" Cassandra's dark eyes lit up. "We get a lot of American tourists here since we're close to the border."

"I bet," said Mackie. "Honestly, though, I never heard of New Brunswick until a few years ago. I just never thought about what was beyond Maine. And now here I am."

"So you're here because you got a house-sitting gig. That's cool," said Cassandra, sliding out of the booth. "Know anybody in town?"

"You," Mackie admitted with a laugh. "I hope that counts."

Cassandra nodded. "Sure it does. And I know everybody. So I can help you meet people. I'd love to go someplace new all by myself. Where nobody knows me."

"It is a little scary but sort of an adventure to be someplace new. Oh, and I have a dog. That's the best part of the house-sitting. The Hamiltons were happy that I was bringing my dog."

Cassandra's face melted into a smile. "Oh, a dog! Can I come by and see him?" Mackie nodded automatically. However as Cassandra stood up to leave, she thought, *Oh, no. What have I done?*

As if she could read her mind, Cassandra bent down, getting in Mackie's face. "Don't worry. I won't make a pest of myself. My mother tells me I have lousy boundaries, but I won't impose myself on you." She grinned, stood up, and called out, "Okay, who needs coffee?" to the nearly empty room.

Unseeing, Mackie stared at her laptop. She touched the remaining bits of sugar on her plate with a fingertip and delicately licked it. Then she drained her coffee mug and folded her computer to leave. She had made one contact and Cassandra had alerted some other people to her presence. That was a lot for a first day.

MACKIE FOUND THE LOCAL grocery store and gathered enough supplies for a few days. When she got back to the house, she realized it was hers, at least for now. Home-for-now. Murphy had been in charge for a few hours. He was dancing with joy to see her and to get outside. They set off up the hill through the evergreen forest, the just-in-case leash looped around Mackie's neck, dog treats in her pocket, and a water bottle in her hand. Walking uphill as the day warmed made Mackie warm, too. Soon she had removed her sweater and wrapped the sleeves around her waist. Murphy was attentive to everything, bouncing from place to place, but Mackie kept walking one step after the other up the hill, letting her thoughts flow along with her body.

Cassandra had appeared friendly, but how much of that was about pumping Mackie for information? What would she be doing now with her knowledge of Murphy or about Mackie being American? Mackie could feel her insides wanting to curl up and hide, but she kept on walking, walking up the hill through the piney aroma of softwood trees. What about those men who now knew there was a new girl in town sticking around, someone not a tourist? What about that guy on the end who had waved to her? Why were they even interested? Why would they care?

Mackie remembered things Sarah had told her. *Small towns are different*, she'd said. *Small towns are places where your business is everyone else's business, too. That's why we live in Boston, girl. We keep to ourselves here.*

Thinking about Sarah reminded Mackie of other things. She felt the cramp of guilt in her belly whenever she thought of her mother. Gone now, Sarah was gone, and Mackie remembered staring at the Charles River, the single sculls flying over the rippling surface, hearing the birds, and the talk and laughter of other people, as if it had been a normal day. All the while she had sat shaking and terrified, knowing that her mother lay dying in a tall building behind her. Mackie remembered her immobility after running out of the building and down to the water. Numbly she had watched the water and heard the sounds, but she'd taken none of it in really, just sat frozen on a bench, wishing to be on another planet, maybe. Or living another life, one in which she and her mother were watching the river together. And while she was at it, why not imagine a life in which her mother was healthy, her ex-husband wasn't controlling, and she was still pregnant?

The cramp in her belly abruptly turned to nausea. Mackie turned off the trail and bent at the waist, retching. The wave passed and she shook herself and washed out her mouth with the water she carried. *Well*, she thought, *you can leave the country and go try to live a new life, but your memories come with you.* Resigned, she called for Murphy and turned to head back down the hill to the little house she was calling home-for-now.

She and Murphy spent a few days at home, with brief forays up the hill for adventure, around the yard to explore, and taking lots of time to settle into the new space. Home-for-now was the only home they had. Mackie decided that she would get the most out of it.

AFTER THREE DAYS, MACKIE was ready to venture back into town. She had a mission to accomplish here in Stella Mare and she wasn't getting anywhere sitting in the Hamiltons' house.

She attached the leash to Murphy's collar this time and they set out through her wooden front gate onto the bumpy, cracked sidewalk. She turned down the hill toward Main Street and the water. They passed a few charming little old homes in various states of disrepair and headed toward the business district. One huge old house caught Mackie's eye with its wandering towers and broad, though decrepit, front porch. A faded sign identified the Stella Mare Inn. The grass was long, full of wildflowers, and the windows were shiny clean. Pots of red geraniums had been set on the porch as if to belie the broken boards and peeling paint. The entire town seemed to have this kind of feeling to it: fading glory, but still radiating charm and care. Closer to the storefront area, traffic increased. Mackie peered through the windows of the Sunshine Diner and caught Cassandra's eye. Cassandra waved and headed to the door.

"Oh, this is your dog!" Cassandra rubbed Murphy's ears.

"This is Murphy." Mackie noted that Murphy was sitting and soaking in the attention.

"Oh, what a good boy!" Cassandra gushed. "Aren't you a handsome fella?" She looked up at Mackie. "I told you I love dogs, right?" Mackie nodded; that was obvious. "Oh, look, Declan!" Cassandra called to the man leaving the diner. "This is Murphy. Isn't he great? And this is Mackie, the girl I told you about."

Mackie's insides curled up in a ball, but she looked up at the man who nodded to Murphy and reached out his hand to her. Tall, he had dark hair and deep brown eyes in a tanned face. With a kind smile, he looked incredibly familiar. Switching the leash to her left hand, she reached back and let him take her hand in his. Oh, yes, this man. This was the man who waved to her the first morning she was at the diner on three hours of sleep. His hand felt firm and strong and warm. And very good. Quickly she pulled her hand away. Very good was unexpected and unwanted.

"Hello," she said quietly and then patted Murphy, looking down. What had Cassandra told him about her?

"So," Cassandra went on, "what are you guys doing? Walking? Have you been down to the docks yet?"

Mackie opened her mouth to reply, but Cassandra went on. "The docks are great if you like fishy smells, slimy places, seaweed, too many gulls. You know, all that stuff that tourists like, but I don't know, do you? Oh, I'm doing it again, aren't I?" Cassandra grimaced and looked at Declan.

He grinned at her. "Yes, Cass, you are. You never give other people a chance to answer. Let's let Mackie say something." They turned identical smiles on her.

"Ah, yeah, I was going to go to the docks," she started. "I want to..." She stopped suddenly, deciding she need not explain anything. "Yes, the docks."

Declan said, "Okay then. That's where I'm headed, too. Let's send Cassandra back to work and I'll take you down. That is, if you want me to." He looked at her carefully.

How could she refuse at this point? They were going in the same direction. Moreover, he knew where he was going and she did not. It would be foolish to not take him up on the offer. But the memory of feeling his hand on hers was still with her and she continued to feel a little like running away.

"Okay, guys, see you later." Cassandra turned back into the diner where at least one person was holding a cup up in her direction. She waved and smiled at Declan and Mackie before grinning at her irate customer and soothing her with more coffee.

Mackie gave Murphy a tug and followed Declan. Mackie felt her initial discomfort evaporate as she fell into step with him, walking the length of Main Street toward the water. It surprised her to feel so comfortable with a man she had just met.

"Cassandra is a funny kid," Declan said. "She's actually my cousin, second cousin, or something like that, on my mother's side. You might notice a family resemblance."

Mackie gave him a sidelong look. "Well, maybe a little. You don't talk as fast."

He laughed. "No, but I probably talk just as much. And I ask a lot of questions, too, so I should tell you right up front that you can just tell me something is none of my business and I'll do my best to stop. I studied journalism and I teach English at the high school. Asking questions is how I find out about people and I really like to know about people."

"Really?" Mackie felt a little overwhelmed. "Why do you care?"

"I don't know. I just think—I know—that people are the most interesting thing on the planet. Well, maybe not to everyone but to me. I just really enjoy talking to people, learning about people. I like my kids at school, and I like to help cultivate some curiosity about people."

Mackie thought about this. Maybe other people were interesting, but she knew that she was not. Not at all. Declan sounded interesting, though, with his journalism and teaching and even coming from this tiny little place. She thought perhaps she'd try him out.

"So, tell me about you," she said. He laughed.

"Classic deflection," he identified. "Good job. That's a great way to sidestep my curiosity."

She grinned, appreciating his appreciation. "I'm really not interesting. I came from near Boston to house-sit for a while. My business is entirely online so I can be here and still work. I picked this place because there was a house to stay in." That was not exactly the truth, but it was close enough. "I have a dog." She was stating the obvious, but why not?

Declan smiled at her. He gestured toward the water. "Let's poke around down here a bit. I grew up on these docks. My family, at least a lot of them, have lived by fishing for generations. When I'm not teaching, I hang out here to help my uncles and other fishers out. I can crew on a boat when someone needs an extra body. I'm pretty good with small engines and I mostly like these old guys. Someday I'm going to write a book about the stories from this dock. I figure my summers are research, more or less."

"Fishers?" Mackie queried. "I thought fishers were animals, you know, like weasels."

Declan grinned. "Yeah, they are, actually. I'm surprised you know that. But what I mean is people who fish for a living. Fisher is our gender-neutral term. Most of the old guys will call themselves fishermen, but women fish, too, so I try to use fisher. You know, modern world. English teacher. Keeping up."

She nodded. More new things to learn.

They reached the town dock where some pleasure craft were moored. Declan suggested, "Let's walk down this way to where the working boats come in."

Turning right, they headed farther away from the town center, along the water. The harbor was in a natural cove, with long arms of land curving on either side of the water, the downtown businesses and town dock near the middle. Mackie was aware that she was walking farther away from her house, but the whole town was pretty small.

The sidewalk of the downtown area gave way to a boardwalk along the shore, shacks and well-kept fish houses set between the boardwalk and the water. Soon enough, the boardwalk became a dirt path, meeting with a road coming from the other side of town. Mackie and Declan stopped where the path and the road met. It was a parking lot full of trucks. To her left, Mackie could see a large building built out over the water.

"Look out there." Declan pointed. At the harbor's mouth far from shore, Mackie could see stone jetties creating the channel for boats to slide into safety from the open ocean.

"Those are some huge rocks."

"Yes. Those jetties were built a long time ago. I often think about what it must have taken for people to create this harbor and settle this town. Fishing needs a safe harbor, especially in wild winter country like this, and it must have taken so much to get that rock here, and then to get it piled out there against the waves. But closer in here, we have the fish market, where the fishers sell their catch, and the best fish and chips in town." He gestured toward the big building.

Mackie saw a sign for wholesale fish and seafood. Around the corner of the outside of the market, she could see a red-and-white-striped awning for the fish and chips bar. From the aroma, she guessed that someone was heating the fryers for the day's lunch crowd. She made a mental note to come back for lunch sometime.

Declan led her up a little hill to a rustic bench overlooking the shore beyond the fish market. From here they could see the entire harbor. Murphy gratefully collapsed near her feet.

"Look over there." She followed his gesture to the left past the big building and the smaller boat and fish houses to the pleasure craft moored close to the main street area. "It's early, so the pleasure boats are mostly still here. But if you look out here, right in front of us, you can see the moorings for the fishing boats. They're out working now, but soon will come back in to drop their catch and clean up for the day. Fishing happens early in the morning, mostly, depending on tide and weather."

Mackie nodded. "That's why the diner is open so early, right? My first day here I woke up at five without coffee and figured I'd never find any."

Declan grinned. "And you were wrong. Sonny opens up at 4:40. He fills thermoses and hands out sandwiches and feeds the breakfast crowd. Cassandra doesn't get to stay out late like a lot of people her age. She's at work at four a.m. but so are many people around here."

"Well, it's a whole unknown world for me," Mackie concluded. "I know nothing about living in a small town, or about living in a fishing town, or anything like that. It's different from what I'm used to, for sure."

"Well, it can have its charm," Declan said, "but it also is a very hard life. There's a lot of good here and there's also a lot of not so good, which probably is just like the rest of the world. I try to keep my focus on the part I have some influence over. And right now, I have to get to work. I told my uncle I'd get the fish house all shipshape before they got back this morning. It was very nice to talk to you, Mackie. And to meet Murphy, too." He patted Murphy on the head, tossed Mackie a wave, and headed back toward the fish houses. Mackie felt a sudden chill as he left. Was that a very abrupt leaving? Did she give off some vibe that told him to back off? What just happened here?

Unsettled, she pulled Murphy closer and leaned in to hug him. He nuzzled her and gave her cheek a quick lick. Men. Just like that they were gone. Or maybe it was people in general. Mackie inhaled the comforting doggy smell of Murphy's neck and then got up to trek back toward town and home-for-now.

"HELLO!"

Murphy leaped up from his bed in the kitchen and headed for the front door. Mackie frowned. Who could be here? Didn't people know better?

Cassandra bounded up the steps. Mackie straightened out her face and pushed the screen door open. "Hi, Cassandra. Come on in."

Cassandra was busy greeting Murphy, who leaned luxuriously against her knees as she scrubbed at his ears, back, and hips.

"Sorry to just show up, Mackie, but I don't have your number," Cassandra explained.

"Oh, right," Mackie agreed, noting to herself that she had purposefully avoided sharing her number. "Want some coffee?" She headed toward the kitchen, Cassandra and a blissful Murphy following.

"Wow, nice house," gushed Cassandra. "I don't really know the Hamiltons. They're retired university folk, right? I just know they're from away."

Mackie looked at her sharply. "Is that the dividing line? From here and from away?"

Cassandra laughed comfortably. "Yeah, I guess so. But it's not as bad as it sounds. It's not like we don't let anyone in, you know."

"Apparently. If the Hamiltons have been here for years and they're still 'from away' it might mean something though."

"Yeah, I guess you're right. I actually really want to go away and be somebody from away. I can't wait until I get to do that." Cassandra sat at the kitchen table, looking at the table and smoothing the cloth under her fingers. Mackie sat, too, after pouring their coffee. This was the first time she'd seen Cassandra any way but utterly confident and outgoing.

"What are your plans, Cassandra?" she asked gently. Cassandra looked up.

"Art school. In Nova Scotia," she said. "But I tried already and didn't get in. I have to keep working. And working to get accepted."

"What's involved?" Mackie asked with genuine interest. "I know nothing about going to art school."

"I need to work on my portfolio," Cassandra said. "I haven't got much experience with any kind of medium at all yet, but I just love making designs and images and working out how to make people really SEE something. I think art school would help me get better at how to do that. So I am taking some classes, and doing a lot of work, actually, around my job. I wish I had more time for art. But I need my job to keep my place and you know, on and on. So that's about me. What about you? What are you doing on that laptop?" She gestured to the table in the windowed corner where Mackie had set up a makeshift workstation near the coffee.

"I did an English degree, actually," Mackie admitted, "which is a fast track to underemployment, but I have a small business where I work as a virtual assistant and handle social media for a few companies, and I do some writing assignments when I get them. I've been working like this for about ten years now, so I have regular clients and regular work. I don't make a lot, but it is flexible and online, so that means I can be here and still keep my job. I just have to be organized and focused."

"What a good system," mused Cassandra. "You're not going to work at four a.m. every day either."

Mackie laughed. "That must be a pretty hard part of your job."

Cassandra nodded. "I don't love that part. But the work is okay, and I like my customers and a lot of them I've known forever, anyway. Or they're related somehow to my family. The old guys, especially, they act like I'm about eight years old sometimes and I have to get 'em to knock it off."

Mackie's mind was racing. Should she seize this opportunity to check out her possible connection to the community? Cassandra was young and talkative, but she seemed to mean well and she certainly knew a lot of people. Mackie looked down at her cup as she considered this big step.

"So," Mackie said slowly, raising her eyes to Cassandra's, "one reason I picked Stella Mare was because I might also be related."

Cassandra's eyebrows went up. "Oh, yeah?"

"Yeah," Mackie repeated slowly. "My mother—my mother always said I had a cousin here."

"Yeah? What's your mother's name?"

Mackie shook her head. "Not through my mother. Through the other side. And my mother's—gone."

Cassandra's face darkened. "I'm so sorry about your mum. But who are you kin to? I don't even know your whole name."

Mackie said, "Brown. My name is Mackenzie Brown. Mackie for short. But I think I might be related to Johnsons."

"Johnsons? There's lots of Johnsons around here. What's your connection?"

Mackie paused. What could she say? Well, in for a penny, in for a pound, her mother always said.

"Here, let me show you something."

Mackie searched through a manila envelope from her workspace and pulled out a small snapshot. With some trepidation, she handed it to Cassandra.

"Who am I looking at?" Cassandra asked. The photo was grainy and well-thumbed; the edges were fraying and bent.

"It's my mother in Bar Harbor, Maine, in the eighties. With a person who could be, well, a relative. A—a cousin."

Cassandra shook her head. "I'm terrible at this, Mackie. I can never recognize somebody I know as old from early pictures. He's probably one of the fishermen. But I think my mother could probably help. She's pretty old, you know."

Mackie wanted to grab the photo back. What had she been thinking to share this much with a girl she barely knew? It was hard enough to talk to Cassandra, the young, nosy, knows-everyone server. Bringing other people in, well, that felt even more risky. The more people knew, the more likely they were to tell her to shove off. "That's okay, Cassandra. I don't want to bother anyone."

"Well, I don't think it would be a bother, honestly, but okay," Cassandra agreed, handing back the photograph. "Hey, do you want to go to the farmers' market this afternoon? I promised to pick up some stuff for the restaurant."

Mackie breathed a sigh of relief. At least she wasn't going to be pressured to meet anybody else. She shook her head. "No, thanks. I have to power through some work here. Maybe a different time." She took a deeper breath and exhaled out some of her anxiety. "And Cassandra?

Maybe don't tell anybody about my cousin thing? I'm not ready to talk about that." She felt heat in her face.

Cassandra looked at her curiously, but then smiled easily. "No problem," she said. "I might talk too much and have bad boundaries, but I can keep quiet when asked."

Mackie ushered Cassandra out with goodbyes, turned the lock, and slumped against the door. What had she been thinking? She felt invaded, as if her sheltered space had been infiltrated by dangerous beings. Could she really trust Cassandra to keep quiet? What would Cassandra do with her information? Cousins on the other side. Mackie mentally kicked herself for being so weird. *Why can't I just say "on my father's side" like a normal person? This is too hard. I don't know what I think I'm going to accomplish here.*

She went into the living room and curled up on the couch. Murphy joined her in the corner where she felt safe and protected. She pulled the blanket over both of them and held on to her dog until her heart rate slowed. *All I want is to have a family*, Mackie thought to herself.

"Hey, Murphy, we're just looking for our family, right, buddy? We've lost ours, what little we had, and we need to check out every possibility while they still exist. Maybe there won't be an option here, but if I don't check it out, I will live with regret and I already have enough of that." Murphy groaned and rearranged his legs to settle more deeply into the cushions.

Her dog was definitely a comfort, but he had little wisdom to offer. She sniffled into his soft, furry neck.

"Oh, Mama," Mackie cried out quietly. "What would you tell me to do? You said he didn't want us and that's why I never saw him. You said he didn't want us and so we stayed away from everyone, stayed in Boston, stayed alone without all the connections that these people here seem to have. You told me over and over that there is no point in trying to connect, that you just get rejected. And now you're dead and I don't have anybody. I have to try, Mama. I know you think I'm wrong, but I have to try. I want to hear it from him." Overcome with crying, Mackie sobbed while Murphy whined and licked her cheeks.

New Girl in Town

Even though she felt safer staying home, Mackie decided to become more visible in Stella Mare. The first step was to become a regular at the diner when the fishers were having morning coffee.

Despite her misgivings, she headed down at five thirty every morning and settled into the booth that she claimed for herself and opened her laptop. She found she could observe surreptitiously while looking like she was busy at work.

On the fourth morning, a gray bearded man in a ball cap called out to her from the front counter. "Hey, Missy! Yeah, you in the red sweatshirt. Whatcha doing there?"

His neighbor elbowed him. "Leave her alone, Jim. Person's got a right to have breakfast without having to talk to the likes of you."

Mackie didn't know where to look. She was sure her flaming face made it clear she'd heard and was ignoring them. Cassandra came to the rescue.

"No harassing my customers, Jim. You can wave and be polite."

"Yah, yah," Jim muttered. He waved at Mackie and she fluttered her fingers back. "Didn't mean to harass ya there, ya just make me some curious."

Cassandra looked up at Mackie then turned back to the men at the counter. Pouring more coffee, she said, "That's my friend Mackie."

Sonny came out from the kitchen. "What's going on?" he inquired.

The cluster of men at the counter laughed and one gave Jim a push in the arm. "Yeah, me and the guys were just wondering about your customer in the back there, Sonny."

Sonny looked stern. "You be pleasant and we all get along fine, Jimmy, you know that."

Something happened to Mackie in that moment. She felt herself shrinking deeper into her booth, trying to hide behind her laptop, but a part of her was saying, *Now, do it now. Get up and do it now.*

Somehow she rose to her feet and walked toward the front of the diner. She slid onto a stool around the corner from Jim, with Cassandra and Sonny on the other side of the counter. Cassandra gave her a grin and set a cup of coffee in front of her.

"Hi," Mackie offered quietly. "My name is Mackenzie. Mackie for short."

Jim looked taken aback. His neighbor grinned at his discomfort and looked directly at Mackie. "Nice to meet you, Mackie," he said. "My name is Russ Johnson, and this lout is Jim. He's got no manners, but he's a pretty good guy."

Jim was still silent.

"You're a Johnson?" Hearing the name stunned Mackie. "I might be related to some Johnsons." Could it really be this easy?

"Oh, yeah, there's a whack of Johnsons 'round here," said Russ. "In this neck of the woods, if you're not a Johnson, you can probably swing a cat and hit one."

Neck of the woods? Swing a cat? Did people really talk like that? Mackie was awestruck.

"So just because a person is named Johnson doesn't mean it's a relative, I guess," she tried out.

Jim found his voice. "I hope not," he said. "Some of them Johnsons are a piece of work."

Russ elbowed him again. "Takes one to know one. Hey, Mackie, nice to meet you. We've gotta get to work. I promise this guy won't be bugging you again."

Jim nodded and tipped his cap to her. There was a general scramble to pay bills and head out the door. Mackie returned to her booth with relief and not a little excitement.

What had she done? And wow, her gamble to open up had really worked.

BEING A REGULAR AT the Sunshine Diner meant that eventually she stopped being an object of interest and blended in with the wallpaper. This meant she could watch and listen and figure things out about this town. One morning, Declan was in again with Jim and Russ. Declan brought his coffee over to her booth.

"May I?" he asked. Mackie tried to ignore her rising excitement.

"Mmm, sure." She gestured to the table. "Help yourself." She folded her laptop closed and looked at him. She decided he was still interesting with his thick, wavy dark brown hair, deep brown eyes, and strong eyebrows like Cassandra.

"You look like Cassandra," Mackie noted. "Did you say you were related?"

Declan shrugged. "Yeah, somehow or other we are. She was a high school student when I first started teaching and that's when I actually got to know her. Being related is pretty common around here."

"I don't have any relations," Mackie confessed, then leaned back. What was it about this man that made her lose her good judgment? She swallowed though and pushed on, feeling the growing need to know more. "That's one reason I'm here. You all are lucky to have so many people who are all part of your family."

Declan shook his head. "Family is as family does. Just being related doesn't mean a lot. I think there is such a thing as a chosen family, too. I've seen that with my kids in school."

"Chosen family?" Mackie inquired.

"Yeah, you know, the people you pull close and stay with. The people you stick it out with, no matter how hard things get. You don't have to have blood in common to have a family like that."

"Do you mean like marriage?" she asked.

"Yeah, I guess so, but not only. Friends who are closer to you than family. People who you count on and who count on you. The ones who stand by even when everyone else leaves."

"Hey, Declan, stop chatting up the girls. Time to get going!" Russ called from where he was standing at the door. Then he waved. "Hi ya, Mackie."

Mackie waved back and Declan got to his feet. "Wait," she said. "I want to know more about this."

Declan grinned and shook his head. "To be continued, I guess. Work calls." He winked and turned toward the door, dropping his cup off on the counter. "Bye, Cassandra. Bye, Mack!" He waved out the door.

Cassandra looked curiously at Mackie; Mackie stared off into space. A chosen family. She had never chosen a family and never looked for family outside of her mother and, of course, Andrew. When she and Andrew accidentally started to create a family, he had been so enraged. The pregnancy ended the marriage.

Divorce, then a miscarriage, followed by Sarah's death, had left Mackie with nobody. Nobody related and nobody chosen. Left alone by her mother, her baby, and her husband, and nobody there to fill in those empty spaces. What if there really was nobody ever again? Would it be possible to make a chosen family?

The cramp returned in Mackie's stomach. That big pain that threatened to tear her apart. She quickly gathered her things, left money on the table, and with a brief wave to Cassandra, she stumbled out the door. She had to get home before the pain overtook her.

Barely seeing the road, she drove home. She stumbled out of the car and into the house. The bright sunshine in the kitchen mocked her.

The warm charm of her safe space felt distant, like she could see it but couldn't feel it.

She went upstairs and closed all the curtains, blocking out the brilliant late June sun. Climbing into bed, she dove under the covers. Let the pain come. Let the racking feelings do their worst. The critic who lived in her head was in full spate. She was a terrible daughter, a terrible wife, and incapable of being a mother. She could not be present for anything important in her life. She had to check out, leave, go away.

She could not stay and fix her marriage. She could only hate her husband for wanting her to give up her one shot at having a family of her own. Then when he left, her body could not hold on to the baby, losing it in a terrible stream of blood, cramping, and terror. She had never in her life felt more alone. After all of that, she could not stay with her mother and at least hold her hand as she was dying. She could only wish that it would be over soon and then hate herself for wishing such a thing.

She had abandoned her mother, her husband, and her child. She didn't deserve to have a family, chosen or otherwise. Being here trying to chase down Eric Johnson, who never wanted her anyway, was a fool's errand. He was right. She wasn't worth the trouble of having her.

Sobs and nausea racked her body. After vomiting, she finally slept long and hard. She got up to let Murphy out and to feed him and returned to bed as soon as she could.

The bedroom stayed dark even though day broke three times before there was a pounding on the door. Mackie ignored the pounding, but she woke up and checked her phone. Three days since the talk with Declan. Three days and most of another one. Whoever it was at the door left, finally, and things were once again quiet.

She climbed out of bed and eased her way downstairs to let Murphy out the back door. Poor pup, he'd been a little neglected. She picked up the manila envelope and carried it to the kitchen table. The afternoon sun was warm. It no longer felt like an accusation, but like a benediction.

Mackie tipped the contents of the envelope onto the table. There was the snapshot with her mother and Eric. There was the silver medallion on a leather thong with a Celtic tree. Sarah had that tucked away with the letters, the picture, and the other things she had never shared with Mackie. The letters spilled out, too, all written by Sarah, an impossibly young Sarah telling Eric about his daughter. Never mailed. The letter telling Eric about the pregnancy, never mailed. No letters back to Sarah. Did he ever know?

Mackie drew a deep breath. She might be all the things that her inner voice claimed or she might not. She could choose to avoid finding out the truth about her father or she could face it head-on. She could be Kenzie, Sarah's daughter, neither of whom felt as though they were good enough to claim a family. Or she could be Mackie, herself, a woman who could make a chosen family even if her biological family was gone or not interested.

This time when a knock came at the door, Mackie answered.

"Thank goodness!" exclaimed Cassandra. "I haven't seen you for days. Everything okay?" Mackie could see her look around.

"It's been a bit of a hard time," Mackie admitted. She might as well, she decided, because the evidence was right there: three days of sleeping in the same rumpled clothes, unwashed dishes, and dog food spilled onto the floor.

Cassandra looked hard at Mackie. "Well, I'm glad you answered the door. You're coming with me to my mum's house for supper. Go take a shower and I'll hang out here with Murph. Go on, Pat is expecting you. Pat is Mum. You'll like her. Go on now."

Mackie was starving, emptied in some deep way, and ready to follow directions. She headed upstairs to the shower and clean clothes. She could hear Cassandra tidying up and talking to the dog. It was vaguely comforting.

When she got back down to the kitchen, combing out her damp hair and looking for her shoes, she slipped the medallion over her head and the snapshot in her jeans pocket. It was time to take a step.

MACKIE AND CASSANDRA arrived with Murphy in Mackie's little Corolla, Cassandra's bike on the back. "What about Murphy?" Mackie asked Cassandra.

"The yard is fenced and Mum's dogs are friendly. You can just let him out if you want. We like dogs around here." She grinned.

"With pleasure." Mackie grinned back. This place already felt welcoming. Murphy bounded off to make friends with the local dogs.

"Come on in," Cassandra encouraged. "Mum's expecting us."

Roses climbed the porch of the little gray cottage, making the little hallway dark, but there was soft music and laughter coming from the back of the house. Mackie slipped off her shoes and put them beside Cassandra's. "Mum!" Cassandra called. "We're here!"

A petite, gray-haired woman in jeans came to the front hall, wiping her hands on a tea towel. "Welcome, Mackie," she said with a wide smile. "I'm Pat. Welcome to my home. I am so glad you're here." Her handshake was sturdy and strong. The welcome Mackie was feeling expanded into a warmth in her belly. Perhaps it was the delicious aromas coming from the kitchen after three days of eating nothing.

"Come in and meet Titus," Pat said. A young man sat at the kitchen table tearing lettuce into a salad bowl. He stood when Mackie came in behind Pat. Cassandra had taken some treats out to the dogs. Titus was tall and appeared a little younger than Cassandra, but he had the same dark brows and eyes as his sister and Declan.

"Hi, Titus," said Mackie. "That's an interesting name."

He laughed. Cassandra came in, adding, "Yeah, Mum is big on Shakespeare. He's only lucky he wasn't Prospero."

"Or Julius," Titus chimed in.

"Romeo?" Mackie offered. They all giggled.

"Are you guys making fun of my baby name project?" Pat demanded with a smile. "I can't help it that the kids were doing *The Tempest* the year that Cassandra was born."

"Mum works at the high school," Cassandra explained.

"Counselor," Pat confirmed. "With a side of drama club."

"Can I help with something?" Mackie asked. "My mother would kill me for coming here empty-handed, so please let me help."

"Sure," Pat said. "Help Titus with this salad and I'll pour us all a glass of wine. I'm looking forward to talking to you, Mackie. Oh, Titus, who else is coming?"

"Nobody, Mum. Everyone else was fed tonight." He grinned at Mackie and explained, "Mum can't stand the thought of anyone going without a meal. I play baseball and she's always trying to get me to bring the guys home to eat."

"We're pretty blessed to have what we have," Pat said, "So I want to make sure we share when we can."

Mackie sipped her wine and smiled to herself. This was pretty nice and she was willing, now, to enjoy it.

After dinner, Pat asked her to bring her tea into the little living room for a chat.

"Come on, Bart, time to move." Pat nudged an old basset hound off the couch to make room for them both to sit. He grudgingly shifted to nap under the coffee table.

Pat smiled at her. "Cassandra told me you wonder if you might have relations here in town."

Full of pasta with marinara, a fresh garden salad, and a slice of cake to die for, Mackie was willing to trust that something good might happen. Pat was a school counselor; she probably really did know everyone like Cassandra had said.

"I haven't even told Cassandra this," she started. "I know who I'm looking for. His name is Eric Johnson. He was probably born sometime in the forties."

Pat looked at her. "And you think he's a cousin?"

Mackie equivocated. "Well, a relative." She pulled the snapshot out of her pocket and handed it to Pat.

Pat looked at it carefully.

"Yes, this is Eric," she said, nodding. Mackie felt a whoosh of relief flow through her. So that picture really was him.

"And who is the girl?" Pat looked inquiringly at Mackie.

"That's, um, my mother," Mackie breathed.

Pat looked at her. For the first time, Mackie realized that her story didn't really hold water. But Pat allowed her to continue the fiction. "This is your mother with your father's cousin, some time ago, right?"

"Yeah, the picture says 1985. And I think they are in Bar Harbor." Mackie's fingers went to her throat where the medallion hung under her shirt. Why on earth would she have a picture of her mother with her father's cousin, when she supposedly didn't know who her father even was? Yeah, the story was pretty thin.

Pat didn't seem bothered at all. She looked completely relaxed. "Well, you probably want to know something about your cousin Eric," she said gently. "Old Eric is quite a guy. He's a great fiddler and he's been fishing most of his life. I know little about his early days. Whether or not my children believe it, I'm a lot younger than the old guys." She laughed.

"Eric went to university; left Stella Mare quite a few times. He has a lot of history. He also has his troubles, Mackie. He drinks too much a lot of time. He has some health problems, and I wouldn't be surprised if he has PTSD."

Mackie wrinkled her forehead. "PTSD? Why?"

Pat smiled. "Well, as you probably know, having traumatic things happen to you can result sometimes in PTSD. Fishing is a dramatic way to make a living. People die, get swept overboard, caught up in ropes, things like that. But Eric has another history, too. He fought in Vietnam for the Americans and I think that was a difficult thing."

Mackie listened and tried to understand all of what Pat was telling her. "Do you think I could talk to him?"

Pat looked at her. "Mackie, I think we both know that you're not talking about finding a cousin. You're talking about something more important than that. Do you know if he knows about you?"

Mackie looked at the floor. This was hard. She looked back at Pat and shook her head. "My mother always said he knew and didn't care. But honestly, when I got old enough to think about it, I figured she just got pregnant and maybe didn't even know who the father was. She kept us away from her family, from anyone, really, and mentioned nothing about him except to say he didn't want us."

She stood up and walked over to the bookshelf, then turned and looked back toward Pat. Taking a deep breath, she said, "But I found some letters and stuff. And that picture. I found all that after she died."

Mackie paused, fondling the medallion under her shirt. Leaning against the bookshelf, she drifted off for a moment. *Oh, Mama, I know I am breaking all of your rules.*

"And?" Pat asked gently after a moment.

Mackie brought herself back. *I'm here*, she thought. *Doing this thing. Keep on going.* She returned to sit on the couch.

"And I wanted to find out. Did he know? Did he reject me? I want to give him a chance, sort of."

Pat looked at her with compassion. "And give you a chance, too, I think."

Mackie nodded. She was surprised at how good it felt to talk with Pat. She had told no one this story, but telling Pat felt okay. It was more than she was a counselor; Pat felt safe, more solid, more secure than Sarah had ever felt to Mackie. Nevertheless, a part of Mackie remained unsure.

Pat seemed to understand that. "Well, it is a big thing. Finding out you have a grown daughter when you didn't know it at all, that can be a big adjustment. You think you're giving him a chance, but first there will be a bit of a shock. You'll want to tread cautiously, Mackie."

Mackie looked down. "I know. And I am so scared that my mother was right, that nobody really wanted us anyway. This entire project might just be a painful extension of that."

Pat looked at her with wisdom in her eyes.. "Keep your own counsel, Mackie. You'll know the right thing to do and the right time to do it. Remember that Stella Mare is a very small town and when you get to know us better, you'll see how everyone is connected, for good or for bad. We take care of our own here."

The thought of taking care—or being cared for—grabbed Mackie by the heart. She could feel her longing to be a part of a community that took good care of each other. Even old Eric with his troubles.

If she had only taken better care of the family that she had before, she wouldn't be here feeling like a complete outsider. If only she had stayed with her mother as she lay dying. She bet people in Stella Mare didn't let their family members die alone. Mackie felt a rising shame and sadness. She turned away from Pat's clear-eyed gaze.

"Mackie," Pat said quietly. "Whatever weight you're carrying, it's okay to put it down and enjoy being here tonight. You're among friends here."

Mackie looked up, nodded, and lifted her chin. Pat was right. She didn't need to drown in the sorrows of the past. It was okay to focus on the present and the future. She could allow herself to be cared for by these people in this moment. She listened to Cassandra and Titus bicker in the kitchen as they washed up. She felt the weight of Bart the basset hound on her foot and the warmth of the teacup in her hand and saw the kindness of the eyes of the woman sitting across from her. A bit of weight lifted as one person in the world knew more of her story. Who knew that telling the story could make you feel better and not worse? Mackie allowed herself to rest for a moment in the relief.

ON SATURDAY MORNING, Mackie was having breakfast at the diner. Cassandra bounced over to her with an invitation.

"Guess what!" Cassandra bubbled. "There's a kitchen party tonight. I'm going. Everyone is going. I think you should go."

Mackie looked up at her curiously. "Kitchen party? What's a kitchen party? Tupperware?"

Cassandra giggled. "No, a kitchen party is where people get together and sing and play music. And eat, of course. And talk and hang out. But it's really about the music. In the kitchen, you know. Although in the summer they're more likely to be outside."

Mackie swallowed the information and shook her head. "That's all new to me," she said mildly. Cassandra really could talk up a storm.

"Oh, and by the way," Cassandra tossed over her shoulder as she went off to fill another coffee cup, "Eric Johnson will be there. You know, your cousin. Your maybe cousin. He plays the fiddle."

Mackie's mind was racing. She stared at the laptop, but she couldn't see the screen in front of her. *Eric Johnson will be at the kitchen party.* Was she even ready to see him? She sipped her coffee, trying to calm her racing mind. What might happen?

A sudden restlessness overtook her. There was no hope for doing any work now. She had to go for a walk or something to burn off the sudden rush of energy. She closed her laptop and started to pack it away. Backing out of the booth, with an armful of jacket, laptop case and messenger bag, she literally bumped into Declan.

"Hello, there!" he said, grasping an elbow to steady her and grinning. "In a hurry?"

"Oh, hi," Mackie muttered, "I'm sorry, I didn't see you."

Declan helpfully took her laptop case in his hand. "I could see that." He nodded. "Where are you off to in such a hurry?"

Mackie stopped and looked up at him. "Yeah, I guess I'm really not running off anywhere in particular." She took a moment to breathe. Slowing down, she once again noticed his soft eyes, strong jaw, and the comforting hand on her elbow. "Cassandra just mentioned something about a kitchen party. I never heard of such a thing and then I suddenly felt like I needed to go for a walk."

Declan laughed. "I'm not sure how one thing follows the other, but I could stand to go for a walk. May I walk with you?"

Mackie's racing thoughts shifted gears. Maybe it would be a good idea to go for a walk with Declan. Maybe he could tell her what to expect at a kitchen party. Maybe he even knew Eric Johnson. Plus, she could not deny that he was attractive. And very nice.

"Okay," she agreed. "Let me dump my stuff in the car though. I don't want to have to carry it."

After unloading her bags and jacket to the car, Mackie and Declan walked briskly away from the docks and toward the town beach.

"So, tell the girl 'from away' what she needs to know. What on earth is a kitchen party?"

Declan laughed. "Kitchen parties are fun. Like good clean family fun. Anyone with any talent or interest brings musical instruments, and everyone sings. The old folks sing old songs and tell old stories. Young folks drink beer and laugh, and everybody has a pretty good time. Even little kids come. Everybody is welcome and everybody has something to contribute. You've never been to a kitchen party?"

"There's not a lot of partying in my history," Mackie noted grimly. "Honestly, where I come from, a kitchen party means somebody's going to try to sell you cookware. This is completely out of my range of experience. Except maybe like summer camp. I went to a summer camp once and there was a lot of singing and playing guitars and such. Are you sure it's okay for me to just show up?"

Declan shook his head at her. "Mackie, did you not hear the 'everybody's welcome' part? You are part of everybody. Everybody is welcome and everybody has something to contribute. Even clapping for the music counts, you know. Appreciation is a big contribution."

She apparently looked unconvinced because he went on, "There's a potluck, usually, too. You can bring food if you don't think you're musical enough to take part."

"Okay." Mackie got it. "I can go to the party, it will probably be fun, and if I bring some food, that'll be good. Right."

"Yeah," Declan confirmed. "A bag of chips, you know. Whatever. Just come. You'll like it."

They continued up the hill, Mackie's breath coming a little faster. She didn't know if it was because of exertion or what she was planning to say.

"You know I'm looking for my relatives, right?" She turned to look into Declan's eyes, feeling a little shock once again at the deep chocolate color.

"Yeah, you mentioned something about that. Think you'll find some at the party?"

She could feel herself tensing up. It was hard to skim around the truth with Declan. There was something so authentic and guileless in his look. "Yeah, well, maybe. I think I figured out that maybe Eric Johnson is somebody I might be connected to."

Declan nodded. "Oh, yeah, old Eric. He'll be there. He's a fixture at kitchen parties. Brings his fiddle. He's getting older but his fiddling is still young."

Mackie felt some of the tension ease in her chest. Pat had said Eric was a fiddler. Cassandra, too. So this guy, this person who might be her father, he was a fiddler, and just maybe, she was going to get to hear him play.

Mackie turned to Declan abruptly. "Ah, I have to go. Thanks for the walk. I've got to get home and get Murphy out for his hike and make something for this party." She started walking down the hill.

"Mackie, wait," called Declan. He jogged a little to catch up with her. "Do you even know where this party is?" he asked her, laughing. "Maybe I can pick you up tonight."

"No!" Mackie almost shouted. "No, that's okay, thanks. Cassandra sent me the address. I think I can find it." She rushed down the hill toward Main Street to her car, leaving Declan looking after her, shaking his head.

"Well, goodbye, Mackenzie," he called after her. She tossed a wave behind her and scrambled for her keys. She didn't know why, but she needed to get home. Away from those deep brown eyes and knowing that she wasn't telling Declan the whole truth.

FINDING THE PARTY WASN'T hard, once Mackie had the right street. Cars and bicycles were everywhere and music spilled from a big backyard filled with light and people. Mackie balanced her plate of caramel squares in one hand as she opened the gate and wandered around the old, shingled house to the backyard. People spread across the wide, low deck and onto the grassy lawn, talking and laughing. On the deck itself, a smiling woman boogie-woogied on an electric piano, while a mixed age group of onlookers sang and clapped and played rhythm instruments. A couple of young children ran past Mackie, nearly bumping into her. Then Cassandra appeared as if from nowhere.

"Hey, Mackie, here you are!" she crowed. "Mmm, what did you bring?" She poked at Mackie's package, lifting the tea towel off the plate to sniff the warm caramel squares. "Oh, yum, those smell great."

"A family recipe," Mackie told her, while looking around distractedly. "What do I do with them?"

"Oh, come on in with me. I'll introduce you to Skerrit and Dee and show you around." Cassandra pushed through the singing crowd toward French doors, opening one side and turning back to hold it open for Mackie. Once behind closed doors the music had muted enough that Cassandra didn't have to shout.

Cassandra pointed and named. "So, that's Bethanne on the piano and Juliet playing guitar. There are others who'll play along, but those two are the main ones. If you have a song to suggest, they can play it! I don't know how they do it, really. Seems a little like magic," Cassandra gushed. "But anyway, let's keep going."

They stepped into a large living room, where small clusters of people were talking, conversation made possible by closing the door on the rocking celebration outside. Making their way through the groups, Cassandra and Mackie headed to the kitchen. The big oak table was spread with all sorts of foods, from meatballs with toothpicks and huge shrimp and dip, to bars and squares of all varieties. A little woman with gray hair, jeans, and pink high-top sneakers was pouring wine.

"Hi, Cassandra," she called out. "Who have you got there? And where's your mum?"

"Hi, Skerrit," Cassandra replied. "I haven't seen Mum yet, but this is Mackie. She's living at the Hamiltons' and visiting from the States. This is her first kitchen party."

"Hi, Mackie." Skerrit reached out with a brown hand to shake Mackie's.

"Mackenzie Brown," confirmed Mackie politely, shaking hands.

Skerrit's smile was warm. "Welcome to Stella Mare and to our home!" She looked at the plate in Mackie's hands. "I see you know the ropes even if it is your first kitchen party. Thanks for contributing to the potluck. Your bars can go over there and the drinks are here, and everything is on a help yourself basis. I'm so glad you could come. Oh, look, here's Dee." A larger and younger woman walked into the kitchen from elsewhere in the house. Her reddish hair was pinned untidily on her head and she looked distracted.

"Yes, I'm here," she said. "Has anyone seen Bruno or Magellan? They took off when the music started and I only hope they're still inside somewhere. Oh, hello. I'm Dee," she said as she noticed Mackie. "I don't think we've met, have we? I might be a bit foggy, though, so just tell me if we know each other."

Mackie grinned despite her own discomfort. This redheaded lady made her feel at home. "Hi, Dee. I'm Mackie, short for Mackenzie. I'm new in town and staying at the Hamiltons'. Who are Bruno and Magellan? Cats?"

Dee continued to look preoccupied. "No, they're rabbits, actually. They're not always super social, though, and I hope they are doing okay wherever they are."

Skerrit shook her head. "Oh, Dee Dee, love, you know they're fine. They manage every time and you worry every time." She walked over to Dee and wrapped an arm around her waist. "No worries, my dear. Let's just have some fun." Dee brightened and gave Skerrit a kiss on the cheek.

"Of course, you're right," she said. Looking at Mackie, she said, "Skerrit is always right. So, who are you connected to? You look a little like the Hamiltons."

Mackie laughed. "Not a Hamilton. I'm from away, actually. Massachusetts." Hmm, Mackie thought, that note of being "from away" might be very useful.

Dee looked surprised. "Bit early for tourists, but welcome anyway. Who brought you tonight?"

Cassandra waved her hand. "Mackie is a friend of mine," she said cheerily. "And Declan's."

Dee nodded. "Well, however you got here, Mackenzie from Massachusetts, you are very welcome. Grab a bite and a drink and let's go soak up some Maritime music." Skerrit took her own glass, grabbed Dee by the hand, and they exited to the deck, leaving Cassandra and Mackie to fill plates and glasses for themselves. Mackie poured a small glass of wine and sidestepped the food.

"You go ahead, Cassandra. I'm not really hungry. I'm just going to keep looking around."

"Okay. I'll be around!" Cassandra pored over the potluck table.

Mackie looked around the house. There were people in the living room playing cards and some more people clustered in the kitchen, glasses in hand, leaning against the counters and deep in conversation. Everywhere there was a low hum of humans connecting, with occasional bursts of laughter, bits of conversation, and the music from the deck outside. Through the big kitchen windows, she could see across the deck into the backyard. There were lights out there, maybe candles, but the sun wasn't all the way down yet, and the space took on a pinkish glow. Across the yard she saw clusters of people, talking, laughing, in motion. Everywhere people were giving and receiving hugs and claps on the back, and small children ran around and through the legs of the adults.

She felt a nostalgia for something, almost like wishing she were a child again, but she had never had a childhood like this. Tears formed as she watched the kids playing silly games in and around the grown-ups, with an occasional adult grabbing one and giving them a hug or a smiling admonishment.

Mackie wished with all her heart that she knew what it felt like to be those kids, secure in their space and community, feeling free to run and play, and knowing exactly who they were. But right now, she was grown-up Mackie at a party. She took a deep breath and turned back toward Cassandra. Time to head outside for music.

Just as Mackie reached the deck and found a space there, the musicians took a break. Suddenly there was more milling around than singing. But the party continued. Groups of people arrived, stuck around for a while, and then left, so that Mackie was aware of the flow of people in and out. She sat on a low bench on the edge of the deck overlooking a perennial border along with a few other people and just soaked in the atmosphere. Mackie felt more than saw Declan as he arrived with a cluster of older men, and she turned away, aware of a wave of heat flowing over her.

Declan headed straight for Mackie, leaving the group behind. She saw him out of the corner of her eye, heading purposefully her way, and turned away to talk to whomever was next to her.

"What do you call these flowers?" she interrupted the middle-aged woman on her left, who was engaged with someone on her other side. Mackie silently hated herself for being rude. *Are you really so scared of Declan that you would boldly interrupt someone with a pointless question? Grrr.*

The woman looked at the flowers absently and said, "I don't know. Skerrit's the gardener; you should ask her." Then she inspected Mackie. "Are you one of the MacPhersons? You look kind of like Janet."

Mackie smiled. "No, I'm from away. Not from here."

The woman frowned. "Well, you could be, you know." She turned back to her other conversation partner as Declan touched Mackie's elbow. She quickly twisted toward him.

"Oh! You surprised me!"

"You surprised me when you ran off this morning. What happened?" Declan didn't look mad, but he looked serious.

Mackie shook her head. There was no point in trying to explain it. She just felt weird when any of this family stuff came up. Truth be told, she felt weird around Declan, although it was weird in a lovely, warm, and melty way. "I don't know. I had stuff to do. I'm sorry. I guess it was kind of rude."

He looked at her and then smiled. "Not rude. Just surprising. As long as I didn't upset you, and look, you got here without my expert guidance, just like you said you could."

Almost against her will, Mackie relaxed into a smile. "Yeah, Siri can get me almost anywhere, even in Stella Mare," she told him with faked confidence. "Why are you so late?"

He shrugged toward the front yard. "Got caught up playing cards with some fishermen and remembered that we needed to make sure Eric got here for the fiddling. Have you seen him? Russ and his brother went off to gather him up."

Eric. The name made Mackie's stomach roil in an uncomfortable but too familiar way. Eric was coming here right where she was. She was going to actually see him.

"Well, I don't actually know Eric, but I don't think they're here yet. You guys were the most recent to show up, at least as far as I know," she said, keeping her voice light. "The potluck table is pretty impressive. Did you want to get some food?"

They headed into the kitchen where the musicians were downing last bites and getting ready to play again. Mackie had seen Juliet during her visits to the Stella Mare library. Tall and wearing her striking ginger hair loosely plaited down her back, Juliet was easy to recognize. She smiled at Mackie as she picked up her guitar and went through the French doors back to the deck.

"Who's ready to make some more music?" Juliet called out to the crowd.

A general cheer went up, and she and Bethanne settled back into their spots, other musicians gathering nearby. Among the crowd of onlookers, people passed songbooks and rhythm instruments, and the singing began anew.

In the kitchen, Declan admired the potluck table and talked. "So, have you ever heard this one?" he asked Mackie, referring to the tune coming from outside. "My dad used to sing this while he was working on his traps, when I was a wee one. Lots of these songs have sad lyrics, but the tunes are lively and fun. It's a weird thing to be dancing a jig to a song about a fisherman dying on the sea."

He grinned at her. Mackie, thinking about Eric, couldn't bring herself to speak.

Declan, obviously trying to keep up the conversation, asked, "So, which chips did you bring?"

Finally Mackie grinned back, despite herself, and shook her head. "My mama trained me better than that. No chips. Homemade caramel squares, right there." She pointed them out.

"Impressive." He grinned. "I myself brought the homemade corn chips and homemade guacamole right from the grocery store." He brandished his plastic bag and pulled out the food. "But I appreciate a woman who bakes, that's for sure. I bet they're delicious."

"You can let me know what you think," she said absently. Her attention was half in the kitchen and half on the deck, listening to the music, but she was also listening hard for Eric to arrive.

A sudden disturbance shifted through the crowd. Someone said, "Here's our fiddler!" and the crowd surged to make room. Mackie tried not to stare out the kitchen window, but her stomach was anxious again. Finally she saw a tall, stooped man in a plaid shirt and ball cap stumble through the crowd and climb the few stairs to join the musicians.

He was bent over as if his back couldn't really hold him and he moved with a bit of a shuffle. But he held his fiddle and bow high in his right hand, up over his head, and a general cry rose up.

"Hey, Eric!"

"Hey, man, we thought you got lost."

"Now we get some good Maritime fiddling."

"Oh, yeah," he said with a short laugh. "You know I'd never leave you without some tunes. I know you need me."

Juliet, holding her guitar, made space and someone brought out a kitchen chair, and Eric sat down. The sounds of fiddle tuning arose.

Mackie went to the window in the kitchen to get a better look at him, but there were too many people. Declan was loading his plate and still talking.

"I want to see this," Mackie said by way of explanation and headed for the door. She slid through and slithered between folks standing on the deck to get to where she could see the musicians, but she herself was out of their view, with all the other folks standing, sitting, and hanging around.

Mackie took a breath and held it. *This is it*, she thought. *Mama, this is the moment. This is my first good look at Eric Johnson*, she thought to herself. *This is my first time seeing him.* She could feel her heart pounding and she wished she'd not had that glass of wine. But it was now or never.

She peered under someone's denim-clad arm and looked toward the musicians. There was Bethanne at the piano, tall Juliet with her guitar, and Eric sat on the chair with the fiddle. He looked bleary-eyed and, as she watched, he wavered a bit on the chair, as if he might fall off. What was wrong with him? How old was this guy?

"Come on, Eric, give us a tune!" shouted somebody. He lifted his fiddle in a small salute and, still wobbling, he tucked the instrument under his chin, thumped his heel authoritatively and started a jig. The piano jumped in and the guitar as well, collaborating. All across the deck and the yard people were clapping and stomping and cheering. The fiddle sang out, loud and clear and compelling, almost forcing Mackie's feet to dance.

Wow, thought Mackie. *Wow, this is Eric. This fiddler who has everyone moving along to the music.* She clapped and bounced to the Irish jig, grinning from ear to ear like almost everyone else. When it was over, there was rousing applause and then only a moment before the trio started again. They played on and on, until somebody asked for a song by request.

As Eric leaned into "Ashokan Farewell," the crowd grew silent. The beauty of the melody, the sweet grace notes, the gentle accompaniment improvised by Bethanne, struck Mackie with a shock of surprise and recognition. This was her mother's favorite song. As Eric's fiddle rippled over the tune, Mackie could see her mother in their tiny apartment, so many years ago, raptly listening to this music from the radio. Mackie felt tears form in her eyes. *Oh, Mama. What I didn't know about you.* But she pulled her thoughts back to the here-and-now. This was Eric. Not only could he make people dance and smile, but he could also do this. Her heart felt very full.

By the end of the tune, people had spread out and she could see better. There was applause and a few catcalls. Eric ignored it. Mackie looked at this man—her father—and tried to take in what she was seeing.

He was old; a lot older than she expected. He also didn't seem well. When he finished the pensive tune, he muttered something to Bethanne and stood up, holding on to her shoulder for balance. He gently set the fiddle and bow on his chair then shuffled toward the house while the guitar and piano took over and the crowd started to sing.

As Mackie watched, Eric went through the open door and toward the kitchen. Someone stopped him to talk and she could hear bits of conversation, but her heart was pounding so hard that she couldn't pay attention. Should she talk to him? Would this be a good time to say something? She started across the deck to the house and slipped through the door. Before she got to the kitchen, she was paralyzed by what she heard.

"Hey, Skerrit." Eric's voice was loud. "Hey, come on over here, girl." Skerrit's voice was a murmur.

"I'm fine, I'm fine, Skerrit, don't need nothing. Well, maybe a kiss or two," he cajoled. "Now I know you play for the other team, but you can still give an ol' boyfriend a kiss."

Mackie could hear as Skerrit demurred. "No kiss, Eric, and I don't think any more to drink. Are you feeling okay?"

Eric was truculent. "No, man, get out of my way. I just need me a little drink, that's all. Just let me get that bottle there."

"No, Eric, I don't think so." Skerrit was firm. "I'm going to find Russ."

Skerrit came into the living room, looking distracted. "Oh, Mackie, hi. I hope you're having a good time. Have you seen Russ Johnson anywhere here? I think he needs to take Eric home."

Mackie shook her head and Skerrit headed outside.

Mackie stood motionless in her place in the living room. What now?

The sound of a crash and shattering glass broke her paralysis. Mackie ran in to see Eric leaning over, arm on the counter and a broken wine bottle puddling at his feet. "What happened? You okay?"

Eric looked up at her. "Damn Skerrit. Stupid woman," he muttered. "Can't get anything here. You! You, girl!" He looked at Mackie. "What are you looking at?" He turned back to the counter and grabbed another open wine bottle. "Where's there a glass 'round here?" he muttered, opening cupboard doors. "Skerrit! Skerrit, where's the glasses? Can't you even give a man a drink when he comes to play for ya?"

If Mackie knew how to disappear, now would be a good time. Instead, she went farther into the kitchen, keeping her eye on Eric and the glass shards and wine spreading across the tile. Maybe she could clean it up a bit.

Russ and Skerrit came back in the kitchen as Eric was pouring a tumbler full of Bordeaux. Mackie watched from her distance.

"Hey, Eric," Russ said jovially. "Having a good time?"

Eric growled. "Wine."

Russ headed to the potluck table. "Hey, Eric, did you have some food? Looks pretty good to me." He put a few items on a plate and took it over to Eric, still leaning on the counter.

Eric shook his head, quieter now. "I'm not feeling great here, man," he said in a low voice to Eric, though his words were still loud enough to carry to Mackie.

"Yeah, I wondered," Russ noted. "Maybe a bite?" He offered the plate. Eric shook his head and took a drink from the tumbler.

Skerrit looked at the floor full of glass and wine, glanced at Mackie, and gestured toward a closet next to where Mackie stood. Mackie opened the closet, pulling out a broom and a roll of paper towels. Skerrit reached for the broom and Mackie wiped up the floor, avoiding the men.

Russ set the plate on the counter and put his arm around Eric's shoulders. He walked Eric toward the table and into a chair.

"What you doing, Russ?" slurred Eric. "I'm jus' having a drink."

"Yeah, man, you are," Russ agreed. "Maybe it's a good time to go home, buddy."

Eric flung Russ's hand off him. "I'm not done playing, Russ. Still gotta do some playing. This lil' girl here, she needs to hear some playing." He gestured toward Mackie, who was on the floor with paper towels cleaning up broken glass and red wine that had spilled like blood.

"Am I right? You need some more fiddling, don't ya?"

She looked up, mute. Eric took a last swig and stood up, stumbling out of the kitchen. Russ walked alongside, barely holding him up.

Skerrit wielded the broom while Mackie finished with the paper towels.

"Mackie, thanks for your help. Come sit with me for a bit." Skerrit led her into a small study at the front of the house far from the crowd. Mackie settled into a wing chair and drew a deep breath, feeling like it had been a week since she last inhaled.

"That was quite a scene for our new guest to witness. How are you doing?"

Mackie nodded. "I'm okay. Thanks."

"Well, Mackie, that's our fiddler. There's no kitchen party without Eric."

"Is he always like that?" Mackie dared to ask.

"Drinking?" Skerrit asked. "Yes, he's pretty much always drinking, but he's not always drunk. I'd say that tonight is not a good night for him. And Russ'll take him home soon enough. Russ watches out for him. A lot of people do, actually. Especially when Kathy's not in town." Skerrit appraised Mackie. "Too much drink is a common enough problem and it's especially common around here. People aren't their best selves when they're drinking, for sure, but it doesn't make them demons necessarily. Was this a first for you?"

"A first? You mean like seeing somebody drunk? No, of course not. I went to college, you know, so I got all kinds of education."

They laughed and Mackie gave herself points for lightening the conversation.

"I was a little scared hearing the bottle break," Mackie admitted. "But it seemed to be an accident."

Skerrit nodded. "Yes, I expect so. He's not feeling good tonight and some times are like that, but he's not generally malicious. He might be an old reprobate, but he's our reprobate, and we do love him, even obnoxious. I'm glad you weren't too shaken up. Have you been enjoying the kitchen party? Except for the obviously ugly parts?" Her smile was warm.

"Yes, for sure," Mackie said. "The music is amazing, and it's been fun to see people from around town at a party. I do like it here."

"That's good to hear," Skerrit said. "I'm ready to go back out there. Are you? If not, feel free to hang out here as long as you want. It's pretty quiet in this space."

"Thanks," Mackie said. "I think I'll stay here for a bit."

After Skerrit left the study, Mackie curled up in the chair.

Her first time seeing someone drunk? No, of course not, Mackie thought. But it was a big first in other ways. It was her first time seeing her father and this was what he turned out to be. A fantastic fiddler. A drunk. A sloppy, obnoxious, hitting-on-his-hostess and also probably homophobic drunk. And old. And maybe more, lots more. This was not the father she had hoped for, but worse, what did it say about her that she was his child?

The music started up again on the deck, but Mackie felt exhausted and a little sick. She collected her dish from the potluck table and slipped out the front door to avoid seeing anyone else. She knew Declan was probably looking for her, or maybe was mad at her for running out on him for a second time in one day. But she could not even think about that, about him. Her mind was too full with Eric.

She dragged her feet as she walked to the car, head down, Eric's slurring voice resounding in her head. *You need some more fiddlin', right, lil' girl?*

Her stomach roiled and she felt like someone had punched her. Home. She just had to get herself home. She pulled open the car door and slid in. Slamming the door on the party, on Eric, on Stella Mare felt better. She didn't need any of it, any of them. Key in ignition, foot on the gas, one step at a time to get home.

MACKIE FINALLY FELL asleep near sunrise and slept through the day. She ignored the knocking at the door in midafternoon and turned off her phone. In the early evening, she fed Murphy, scrounged in the kitchen for tea and toast, and then went back to her bedroom.

The moon rose late, curving into the deep twilight of a Maritime night. Mackie watched it travel across the sky, her legs curled under her, wrapped in a blanket, and her hand twined in Murphy's curly fur. She leaned against piles of pillows on her bed, gazing out the tall windows, watching the night sky and waiting for the morning. Sleep was not to be, much as she wished for it.

Eric. How to make sense of what she thought she knew and what she had learned? Mackie's mind was full of the things her mother had told her.

He never wanted us, Kenzie. It's best to just keep out of sight sometimes and not get yourself in trouble. If you can't be the person they want you to be, then they just leave you.

Was that really what happened with her mother and Eric?

Mackie knew the story Sarah had told her, but she also knew something else, something that had sent her on this wild goose chase to Stella Mare to meet her father. Well, to meet Eric, the man who she thought was her father. Maybe even that wasn't true.

Who is this man, anyway, this old man in a plaid shirt who plays the fiddle like an angel but who can barely walk to his next drink? What does he have to do with me, Mackie wondered, *Mackenzie Brown?*

But Kenzie Brown was the girl her mother had made, all by herself. Raised her alone, keeping her away from anyone who might be family. Told her about life and how to get along with people, and how to keep people at arms' length, or further away. Sarah, the one who kept nobody close except for her daughter, giving advice. Because of Sarah, Kenzie knew that she was expected to accommodate. Relationships were fragile and if you made a single misstep, or let anyone know you needed or wanted something, they would leave you. These were lessons Kenzie learned from a young age.

Mackie remembered herself as the child Kenzie. "Mama, I want more cake." Followed by Sarah's stare and firm words:

"There is no more cake for demanding little girls."

"Mama, can we please get a kitten? I would love a kitten."

"Kenzie, you know we can't have a kitten. They're too much work and besides, they die."

"Mama, where is my daddy?"

"Kenzie, you know we don't talk about that."

"But Mama, everybody has a father. That's how babies happen." Mackie still remembered her mother's furious glare and the way her stomach turned to water as she received it.

"What do you know about babies? Kenzie, your father did not want you and did not want me. He didn't care about us. I wasn't his kind of woman and a baby wasn't what he wanted. I can take care of you. We're a team, Kenzie, you and Mama. We're okay. Mama won't leave you."

Oh, but you did, Mama, Mackie thought. *You did. You died right there in the hospital while I was watching the river go by. You left me. But not without dumping your wisdom on me.* Mackie felt anger course through her. Anger at her mother, her poor, dead mother, but anger for sure.

She remembered her mother's counsel. *Men have needs, Kenzie, and a smart woman pays attention to what he needs instead of what she wants. If you want him to stick around, anticipate his needs. That's what I didn't do with your father. If I had been a different way with him, maybe things would be different.*

"Oh, Mama," Mackie said aloud, "I'd never have married Andrew if you hadn't been telling me to grab on to him, keep him happy, make sure he had a happy wife and a happy life. Look at how that turned out."

Mackie could almost hear her mother's voice. *You sent him away, Kenzie. Remember that. You didn't have to let him leave you. You could still be Andrew's wife.* In Mackie's memory, it felt exactly like, "There is no cake for demanding little girls." Sarah telling her, once again, that she could not have what she wanted and, in fact, should not even want it.

Mackie pounded the bed with her fists in frustration. "Yes, I could still be married, but Andrew couldn't accept a baby! Mama, you never understood that. Andrew didn't want me, the real me, the one that wanted a family and a home and a dog. Andrew wanted the person I pretended to be. The one who went along with everything, even let him pick out my clothes. That's not love, Mama. That's giving yourself away, bit by bit, until it came to the baby. You know I couldn't give up that baby. You didn't give up the baby that you got by accident."

Mackie sobbed with grief and frustration. How could it be that Sarah blamed her for the failure of her marriage when Sarah herself left all her family behind to raise a daughter alone? She might have blamed her daughter for the miscarriage, too, for all Mackie knew.

"No matter how I look at it, in my life, I am the loser. Loser, loser, loser. I lost because you were afraid of your family's judgment. I lost because you were afraid of Eric's rejection. I lost because I followed your rules and gave up on myself. I lost my home, my husband, my baby, and now I even lost you." She collapsed in a paroxysm of sobs, dampening the bedcovers, and prompting Murphy to lick her cheeks.

After a few minutes, the wave of sobbing passed. Her entire life until now seemed like a dream, a long-ago dream full of sadness and loneliness and faded images. A dream from which there was no awakening. Exhausted, Mackie fell into deep sleep.

She woke to wind howling and the pounding of rain on the metal roof of the porch. Letting Murphy out in the yard, she brought her mug of tea to the porch where she settled in the big rocking chair to watch the sheets of rain fall. Murphy came bounding back, curly fur dripping. The wind abruptly shifted direction, sending showers into the porch. She and the dog went back inside where Mackie grabbed towels to rub down Murphy's coat and her own hair. A rainy day seemed just right. Nobody would come calling, nobody would ask her to go for a walk or a bike ride, and she could just continue to stay here and sort through her thoughts.

Somehow the wind and rain brought a sense of purposefulness. She fed the dog and went to her worktable in the kitchen. The big manila envelope where the snapshot lived had other items inside. Mackie dumped out the small pile of letters and a notepad, determination in her jaw.

"Well, Murph, I'm here and he's here. He might not be who I want him to be, but he might be able to help me know more about who I am. There's nobody else at this point." Murphy was busy with his meal but glanced at her as she spoke.

Mackie laid out the letters and the snapshot and dumped the medallion from the envelope. This was the safe place where she kept it, except when it was around her neck. She hefted the silver disk in her palm, leather thong dangling. She took a deep breath, feeling the weight of the talisman and the edges of the design as her hand curled around it. She felt the impression of the Celtic tree of life on her palm. With a sudden shock, she connected the symbol to Eric's fiddling—those ancient Irish and Scottish jigs and laments. *I wonder if Eric ever played for Mama? Oh! I wonder if he ever played "Ashokan Farewell" for her?*

She felt a sudden stabbing sensation in her heart, as she recalled another childhood lullaby, a wordless tune that Sarah sang. Old music from the Isle of Man, she had explained when Mackie was older. And Mama's collection of old cassette tapes of Celtic music. She maybe even had Eric playing the fiddle on some of them. Eric might have been on those old tapes. She might have had more of Eric than she realized. Mackie could hardly catch her breath.

Still gripping the medallion, she ran her thumb over the engraving once again. "Bar Harbor, 1985. May love last forever."

Turning to the snapshot, she looked closely at the couple. Yes, there it was, the very medallion on his neck, or maybe that was just her imagination. It was pretty hard to discern details in that grainy photo. But no, she was sure she was right. This was Eric, even though the Eric she met the other night was a far different version. And this Eric was wearing the medallion she held in her hand. This medallion had been her talisman for this crazy real-life adventure ever since she had discovered it among her mother's things. She mused on that day about six months ago, when she was still known to herself and others as Kenzie.

KENZIE WAS CLEARING out her mother's tiny apartment in Somerville. Her mother had been dead only a week, but it was close to the end of the month and there was a new tenant ready to come in. The late December sun poured through the window into the bedroom where Kenzie was pulling out clothes, old suitcases, and boxes of paperwork from the closet.

She felt like an automaton, doing what had to be done because there was nobody else to do it. She piled clothes into bags for donations, sorted papers into the garbage can, and gently fingered her mother's meager collection of jewelry. A pair of pearl earrings that Sarah received at age sixteen, Kenzie remembered, and a couple of religious medals, plus Kenzie's own Girl Scouts insignia. That was about all that was in Sarah's little wooden jewelry box. Kenzie tucked them into her jeans pocket and put the box in the donation pile.

Turning to a box of papers, she sorted and discarded old electric bills, canceled checks (who still used checks?), and birthday cards that Kenzie herself had given to her mother. Those she put in a pile to keep though she couldn't imagine why. She just knew that she wasn't trashing them, at least not today.

At the very bottom of the box was a big envelope. Inside, Kenzie found her birth certificate. Oddly, she'd never needed to look for it before, but here it was. She felt a familiar annoyance when she looked at the names of her parents: Sarah Brown and Unknown. Kenzie knew her mother. She knew perfectly well that her father was not unknown. What must it have taken for Sarah to make that claim, knowing that people would assume she had been sleeping with so many men she didn't know who the father was? Kenzie shook her head in wonder. What motivated her mother was still a mystery.

Kenzie added the birth certificate to her pile of items to keep. The last item in the large envelope was another envelope, stuffed with papers. She dumped the contents out on her mother's mattress. Letters! Unopened, sealed, and in some cases, even stamped, all addressed in her mother's handwriting.

Her breath caught in her throat. More of the mystery. She sat on the edge of the bed and picked up one envelope. Her mother's handwriting, for sure, and the return address was in the North End of Boston, a place Kenzie vaguely remembered as a home they'd had for a brief time. She picked up another envelope: return address was different, but it was another address she'd had with her mother. The addressee in both cases was the same. In fact, as Kenzie poked through the letters, she discovered that the addressee was always the same: Mr. Eric Johnson, Stella Mare, New Brunswick, Canada.

She looked in the big envelope. There was a photo stuck in the bottom. When she pulled it out, she felt wonder and irritation together. That was her mother, certainly, much younger. Very much younger. And a man, a man much older than her mother but still handsome. He had his arm casually draped across her mother's shoulders, and they were both laughing. Kenzie turned the snapshot over and saw her mother's handwriting. Bar Harbor, July 1985.

There was something left in the big envelope. Kenzie stuck her hand in and felt around. Tissue paper, it felt like, with something hard inside. She slid her hand out, holding the object. The tissue paper was yellowed and crackly, and fell away easily. A medallion. She smoothed her fingers over the Celtic design. She felt the edges against her palm. She stroked the leather thong that made it a necklace. She noted the engraving: May love last forever.

Suddenly overwhelmed, Kenzie stuffed the medallion, picture, and letters back into the envelope, tied it closed, and carefully added it to her "keep" pile. Giving it a longing look, she returned to clearing out her mother's apartment. This mystery would have to wait until she had a little time to think.

Kenzie could barely recall the truck arriving from the donation center to pick up her mother's things, could barely remember turning in the keys to the building superintendent. She could barely remember much about those days and nights after her mother died anyway. But she easily recollected finding those letters and her memory of the night she opened them was precise and detailed. She could remember everything. As if she sensed that the contents of those letters would be important, she set a scene to create a memory.

In the kitchen of the small house she had shared with Andrew, she carefully set the table for dinner for one. Murphy was curled up on his dog bed, overseeing the proceedings from a place of comfort. Kenzie lit candles, poured herself a glass of wine, and turned on some music. On the table lay the medallion, the letters, and the snapshot. She looked at the dog. "Well, Murph, it's time to see what my mother had to say to Eric Johnson. Are you ready?" Murphy indicated his readiness for sleep, but Kenzie was intent.

It wasn't hard to imagine who Eric Johnson might be, especially when you think about dates, Kenzie considered. "Mama worked in Bar Harbor as a server during the summers from the time she was old enough until she became somebody's mother," Kenzie told Murphy. "My mother," she amended. Then she laughed at herself. "You don't care a bit, do you, Murph?" Murphy acknowledged his name with a stretch and a groan. Kenzie felt silly about talking to the dog, but his doggy presence was comforting.

In a rush, she slit all the envelopes and pulled out the contents. Her mother's schoolgirl handwriting was clear, and her carefully formed letters and attention to proper letter format brought tears to Kenzie. How very young Sarah had been! The dates allowed Kenzie to put the letters into a chronological order.

The first letter was on flowered stationery, with a faint fragrance of wildflowers.

August 1985

Dear Eric,

I miss you. I miss seeing you at the restaurant, and I miss walking on the beach late at night, and I miss you holding me, and I miss all our time together. I wish you could come back. I know you have work there. I have to work here and probably go back to school. Maybe I can visit you? xoxo

Love, Sarah

Kenzie felt a twisting in her gut. Poor Sarah, left in Bar Harbor, maybe even in love with this older man. The next letter was different.

September 1985

Dear Eric,

I am scared. My period didn't come this month, and I don't know what to do. My parents won't be okay with this. I need your help. Please help me.

Next:

November 1985

Eric,

I am having a baby. It is your baby. I wanted us to be together, and I didn't expect a baby, but now I have this thing happening. I need your help. I don't think I can do this alone.

June 1986

Eric, this is to inform you that you have a daughter. Mackenzie was born on April 15, 1986. She is beautiful, so beautiful, and you'd be able to see her if you would only get in touch. Also, you need to send child support.

April 1990

Eric, she is four years old. You have taken no interest in me or in her or in anything. You are missing out.

June 2004

Eric, I have raised this child on my own. All by myself. With no help from anyone, not my parents, not my sister, and not you. She is a wonderful girl and a good daughter. She graduated from high school tonight, and you were not here. I am proud of her and proud that I could do this on my own. I didn't need you after all.

And the final letter, dated in the last year:

A TALISMAN OF HOME

September 2014

Dear Eric,

I am probably not going to live a lot longer. Even though you don't deserve it, I have never stopped thinking of you. I couldn't, because I had this beautiful Kenzie here to remind me of that summer we spent together. From where I sit now, I can see how my fear kept me from taking risks. I didn't allow myself to contact you, except in my imagination. And in my imagination, you rejected me, over and over. The way I felt after you left Bar Harbor that summer was so awful, I couldn't risk feeling that way again. Rejected, you rejected me and you rejected Kenzie, both of us.

Now I can see that I was the one who rejected. I rejected any possibility that you could have been something to me and to our daughter. It is only now that I can understand that I was too scared to mail these letters. And I am still too scared. I won't mail this one either. I have never told Kenzie about you or about that summer. I have only told her that men reject women like us and that she needs to plan to take care of herself unless she can make Andrew happy. I wish I could have kept you happy, but now I understand that I didn't even dare to try. I am so sorry.

Kenzie's wine went untasted on the kitchen table. She tried to imagine her mother full of all those feelings. All of this had been happening inside her mother's stiff, rigid outsides. She had been in love, she had been wanting, but she had let no one see those parts of her. Not even her supposedly beloved daughter.

Kenzie suddenly noticed how still she was holding herself, feeling as if she might shatter. What to make of all of this? She felt such overflowing sadness for her mother. How sad to live and die like that, without daring to reach out. Underneath her sadness, Kenzie could also feel some excitement. With a sense of wonder, Kenzie allowed herself to think about Eric. Yes, she had a father. Yes, he had a name and a town. And no, he never rejected her because he never knew she existed. At least that's what the stack of unmailed letters suggested.

Eric Johnson. He never had time to reject her. Her mother tried so hard to protect herself and Kenzie from certain rejection, she never took the chance to see if it would really happen. As the excitement built inside her, Kenzie had to get up from the table, had to move her arms and legs. She called to Murphy and grabbed his leash. She was awash with a great restlessness and had to take some action. This was big news. It meant something. She and Murphy walked for miles and miles that night until Kenzie was spent.

She had never before felt so called to action. Even separating from Andrew was in reaction to his demands rather than active engagement. Something new was moving in Kenzie Brown, and she felt determined to follow it up.

During that snowy walk, Kenzie made some decisions. Her mother may have died with regrets, but that was not for Kenzie. Risks are risks, and yes, she knew that she feared a lot of things, but there wasn't much left for her in the life that she once had. When you have lost everything, you have only two choices. Curling inward and waiting to die was not the one she chose.

Instead, she decided on a new self, a new life, and engaging in an adventure that might, possibly, lead her to having a family. That night she stopped being Kenzie, the girl who did what Mama said, and became Mackie, the woman who had survived so many losses that she no longer feared rejection.

I am Mackenzie Brown, she thought. *I am Mackie Brown, daughter of Sarah Brown and Eric Johnson. And I am going to find my father.*

MACKIE SAT IN HER BORROWED kitchen in Stella Mare. She remembered the feeling from that wintry night when she first discovered that she might find her father. She remembered doing online searches for his name, checking death notices in fear that he had died before she got to meet him. He was very much older than her mother, after all. She remembered the effort it took to find this house-sitting gig and selling her old house to help finance the trip. She remembered, with a wash of shame, how angry she felt with her mother just today. Poor Mama. What a terrible wasted life.

And here she was, and here Eric was, and he was not the father she wanted him to be. He wasn't the person she wanted him to be. She tucked the letters back into the manila envelope. She had no need to reread. They didn't tell her any more about Eric.

Eric Johnson. Old, sick, drunk but a dab hand with the fiddle, as Pat had noted ironically. And much loved, or at least cared about, in this community. *He must have some redeeming qualities besides fiddling,* Mackie thought grimly. *I wouldn't pick him for a friend, that's for sure, but still. You don't get to pick your relatives the way you pick your friends.*

Besides, if I leave now, I'll just wonder forever whether we could have connected. And I will still be a loser, without ever finding out if it could have been different. Mama never could give him a chance. Maybe I can, she thought, as she slipped the medallion over her head and tucked it inside her shirt. *He might not want a chance, but I can offer it.*

Winning Eric

The rainy weather held for four days. By the fifth, both Mackie and Murphy were done with it. When the sun came out and started to warm the wet trees, mist filled the piney woods behind the house. The pair took a long hike up the hill and across into the grassy pastureland on the plateau above the coast. By the time they got home, they were both ready for a big lunch and afterward, Murphy headed to bed for a nap. Mackie headed downtown to the docks.

She parked near the fish market and gathered her courage. Wandering along the boardwalk, she checked out the fish houses. The large one was on the far side, beyond the fish and chips stand. Smelling the aroma, Mackie momentarily regretted having already eaten. Next time, she told herself, and headed past the striped awning to the big fish house down the shore. She pulled on the screened door that attempted to keep flies out. She heard men's voices inside. She poked her head in.

"Hello?" her voice wavered.

"Hey, lookit, it's the little girl from Massachusetts," somebody said. "Come on in. We don't bite." She stepped in, letting the screen door close softly behind her.

"Hey, let that door slam!" said somebody she recognized from the kitchen party. "That's how we know somebody's here!"

Another grizzled fellow laughed at him. "Her mama taught her manners, Dave. Be nice."

Dave laughed, too. There were about five of them in the fish house, three sitting around a table near the back wall, holding playing cards.

Dave was standing, leaning against the wall, holding a paper cup of coffee. He grinned easily at Mackie and she grinned back.

"What are you doing here in Stella Mare if you're a Boston girl?" he asked cheerfully.

"Oh, you know," Mackie said. "Something new and different." He seemed satisfied with that.

Mackie saw Russ at the table with the cards. "Oh, hey," he said. "How you doing, Mackie? You were at Skerrit and Dee's kitchen party, weren't you? I thought you were there with Declan."

Mackie frowned. "I was there, yes. It was my first kitchen party, you know, being from away."

Russ laughed. "Oh, right, from away. How'd you like it? Pretty fun, right?"

She nodded. "Yes, pretty fun. What goes on here?" She turned the topic away from herself and the kitchen party. For the first time, she realized that Eric was one of the men at the card table. He was silent, turned in on himself, but then she realized that he was paying attention to something in his hands. As she watched out of the corner of her eye, she saw him pull a flask out of his hip pocket and doctor his coffee cup.

Russ explained about the fish house. "This old place isn't used for much anymore. It was Eric's dad's place back in the day. We mostly show up here to drink coffee and shoot the breeze. If you want to see a real working fish house, come on over to where we clean our catch and bait traps down the boardwalk. That good-looking Declan Kelly, he's likely to be there, too."

Russ gave her an arch look. Mackie tried to stem the flush that she knew was rising in her face, but all she could do was ignore the reference and ask a question.

"What do people fish for here?"

"Oh, well, lots of things. The Bay of Fundy is a mixed fishery." Russ settled in to explain. "Some folks fish lobster; that's what those big wire traps are for. Some of us use weirs or nets to catch a mess of little fish, like gaspereau. There are lots of ways to catch fish, and lots of rules. We're limited in what we can catch and sell, to keep the stocks healthy. It can be pretty complicated."

Another man who Mackie hadn't met added, "Might be complicated, but mostly you just do it. Head out early in the morning, work your tail off to try to catch your fish, bring it in to harbor and try to sell it. Hope that weather or some whale don't make you shut down the whole business. It's just work." He looked at her curiously. "You a reporter or something?"

Mackie laughed. "Nothing like that. I know nothing at all about fishing for a living and since I'm in Stella Mare, I thought I might try to find out."

"You watch out for that Russ feller there," the man said. "He's the one knows all about fishing here. He'll talk your ear off, that one will."

Russ laughed and nodded. Then he turned back to Mackie.

"You know, Declan knows a lot, too. He grew up on these docks; lost his own dad to a bad storm back when he was just a pup. He's a good feller, Declan is."

Mackie didn't know why people felt the need to keep telling her how wonderful Declan was. She didn't doubt it. She was just on a different mission.

The card game continued along with desultory conversation. Eric, in the corner behind the card table, gestured to Mackie. "Come on over here, girl from Massachusetts. Sit down and tell us about yourself." He pointed to a stool by the bare wood wall.

Mackie pulled the stool out and perched on it. Her heart was pounding, but the new Mackie was determined not to let a little fear get in the way. "So, what do you want to know?" she asked, a little timidly.

"You got a name?"

"Yes, Mackenzie. Mackie. Mackie Brown." She tried to make her voice clear and bright.

"So you, Mackie Brown, what do you think about this hand of cards here? What do you think Sam should do?" Eric was peering over Sam's shoulder and invited Mackie to look, too.

"Hey!" Sam objected, folding his hand. "That's none of your business. They shoot people for less than that, Eric Johnson. Don't you be teaching her none of your cheating tricks there."

Eric cackled and backed away and Mackie, too, slid back onto her stool. Covertly assessing Eric, she scanned for resemblance. Did she have his nose or mouth? Certainly not those steel-blue eyes. Suddenly he turned back to her, with a lift of his chin. "So, you like poker, Miss Massachusetts?"

Poker was a foreign language, just like fishing. "Ah, no. No poker for me. Old Maid, that's a game I know how to play."

He lifted his eyebrows. "So no cards, huh? Too bad."

"Well, cribbage. I can play cribbage. And, you know, Old Maid." He grinned at her and she grinned back. She felt her heart start to pound as she realized she could be looking at her own smile in the mirror. Yes, she had his grin. How could anyone not notice that?

"Okay, then, cribbage. You're a New Englander for sure. Only today it looks like its poker." He nodded toward the table. "You come back another day and we'll play. There's a board here, right here," he said, leaning back and gesturing to the handmade cribbage board hanging on the wall.

"Sure," she agreed, but her mind was racing and she felt a desperate need to get out of the claustrophobic fish house. What did she think she was going to accomplish by hanging out down here? Chastened, she slid off her stool and headed for the screen door.

"Where you off to, girl?" called Eric.

"Gotta go," Mackie said with a little backward wave.

"Come back again," said Eric firmly. "Bring some decent coffee with you next time. We won't have to drink Russ's slop. And we'll play. We'll play crib."

Mackie nodded and escaped into the bright daylight. Letting the screen door slam behind her, she walked briskly toward her car, bypassing the fish and chips once again. Her heart only started to slow as she reached the Corolla. She sighed deeply and turned her face toward the sun, leaning against the warm side of the car. She'd done it. She'd broken the ice. She'd talked to Eric and survived.

IT WAS THREE DAYS LATER, and earlier in the morning, when Mackie returned to the fish house. She carried a cardboard tray with two cups of coffee. The screen door creaked open and she peered in. Quiet today. But there was Eric sitting in what she assumed was his usual seat. His hands were busy with a penknife and a small piece of driftwood. His eyes were trained on the fine detail of his carving. She slipped in, quietly saying, "Hello."

He looked up and there was no recognition in his face. Instead, he looked like he was a million miles away. But then his attention sharpened, and his face brightened a bit.

"It's that Mackie from Massachusetts," he welcomed her.

She felt warmed. "Yes, it's me. I brought coffee. From the Sunshine."

Eric smiled and gestured to her. "Come on over here then and let's have some coffee."

They sat together at the little coffee-ringed table. "So, Miss Mackie, what brings you here?"

"Here to the fish house or here to Stella Mare?"

"Both, maybe. A lot of people come to Stella Mare, but most of them don't come hanging around with the fishermen at the docks. But here you are."

Mackie shrugged. "I work online and sometimes I just need a break. I hope it's okay for me to visit. I did bring the coffee, after all." She looked at his face. "Is it okay? Am I disturbing you?"

"Disturbing? Nah. I'm retired. You can't disturb me. I don't go out on the boats any more, but I like it down here. This spot right here was my grandfather's fish house. A lot of the guys use it for visiting, not so much for working any more. But the coffee is pretty bad here, so thanks for bringing some."

She sipped at her cup. "What are you carving?"

He held up the six-inch piece of driftwood. It was a boat, or the beginnings of one. "We used to keep our hands busy knitting trap heads, but nowadays I just do this, mostly for fun. Sometimes the tourists like to buy this stuff though," he said, putting the boat aside and picking up his coffee. "You didn't tell me why you're down here at the docks. There are a lot of places to take a break."

"I'm going to be living here for the next year, so I figured I should get to know the people in my new town." Mackie hoped she was convincing.

"Huh. Starting with the oldest person, I guess. What do you want talking to an old guy like me? What do you want to talk about?"

"I don't know, really. Maybe you can tell me about you. Do you like to travel? Do you ever go to Maine?" This was coming close. Mackie could feel her breath getting shallow and her heart racing.

"Oh, yeah, Maine, but that's not traveling. That's right next door. What about Indonesia? Or Europe? How about Australia? That's traveling."

Mackie marveled. "Have you been to all those places?"

Eric laughed. "No, no way. Did a tour in Vietnam when I was a kid and lived in Maine long enough to go to school, but those other places I travel in books. You much of a reader, Miss Mackie? I don't think people read much anymore."

"Well, maybe people don't, but I do, yeah," said Mackie. "Not travel books though."

"I don't read travel books either," Eric agreed. "I read novels set in interesting places, where the writer has done his homework. That way

I feel like I have been somewhere and when I get really interested, I google it and look at pictures. That Google is a pretty good invention."

Mackie laughed. "It sure is. That's how I knew how to find Stella Mare." Oops. She shut her mouth firmly.

"You were looking for it? What are you looking for?"

"Just this town. I liked the name," she said, looking away. "I was actually born in Maine, near Bangor," she added, changing the subject. But maybe this was also too close.

"Is that right? Who are your people? What did you say your family name is?"

"Brown. But my mother died last winter and I never knew my father." She tried to say it cleanly, but there was a little catch in her throat. It was so weird to say that to Eric, sitting right in front of him, knowing what she knew and what he didn't know.

"Well, Miss Mackie, that's some sad. I am sorry about your mum and I am also sorry you didn't get to have a father. I know it's for sure a terrible thing to not have a father. That happened to me, too. I was six and he never came home from a fishing trip."

Mackie looked at him curiously. "You, too? Somebody told me that happened to Declan Kelly, too."

"Oh, it's not an uncommon story around here. The sea takes people. Not always, but betimes. And there are almost always children."

"That's so sad to think of those kids without parents," Mackie said quietly.

"And I guess you're one of us, aren't you?" Eric noted. "But really, why are you here, in Stella Mare? What's a young girl like you doing here? Us who were born here call it home. We love it, but I would think you'd like the city better, being as you're used to that."

"I think I might have some cousins in New Brunswick," she told him cautiously. She studied his face. "I thought I'd spend some time here and see what I can find out. With Mama gone, I don't feel like I belong in Somerville anymore. Or anywhere."

"Ah, that's a wicked hard thing, to not know where you belong," he opined. "I think I've had that feeling more than a few times myself." He looked at her with sympathy. Mackie felt her heart pound as she held his gaze for a long moment. Then she pulled away from those steel-blue eyes.

After a moment of silence, Eric continued, "I hope you find your people, young lady." Then he slid a flask from his pocket and dosed his coffee. "It's a hard thing to be without your family. But this is a hard place to live, too. When late fall comes and there's barely any sunshine and the wind cuts through you, you might wish to be almost anywhere but here, even with family."

She smiled. "Yeah, I know that summer is only part of the picture. It's pretty beautiful right now. But I'll be here for the winter, too. I'll get to find out what I'm made of then, I guess." They looked at each other for a smiling moment.

Eric gestured to the pegboard hanging on the wall. "You said you play cribbage."

"Yes, I do." Mackie said. "That was one thing my mother taught me."

"Come back sometime and I'll give you the opportunity to lose to a world-class crib player."

"Right. I'll be prepared for that." She laughed, then Murphy barked once outside, giving her opportunity.

"That's my signal; time for me to go. My dog needs me. Well, thanks for the talk," she said, standing and gathering her things. "I'll come back again, if that's alright. So you can beat me at crib. And maybe recommend some books."

He nodded, picking up his driftwood boat again. "Don't forget the coffee."

She grinned and gave a brief salute as she opened the door to the brilliant sunshine. As the screen slammed behind her, she grinned to herself and clenched her fist. *Yes! I did it!*

"HEY, DAVE, ERIC." MACKIE tossed off a brief wave as she sauntered to her favorite booth in the back of the Sunshine Diner, laptop bag in hand. Cassandra gave her a grin and a chin up as she poured coffee at the counter. This was feeling almost normal, ridiculously early though it might be. The earlier she was up, the sooner she'd get her work done for the day and then she could focus on her real job: getting to know Eric and this town.

And also Declan. Sort of.

She couldn't help noticing when he walked into the diner. She couldn't avoid how her whole being oriented toward him, even with Eric in the restaurant. Declan noticed Mackie, too, as he waved to the guys but came first to her table.

"Hey, there," he said. "Can I sit for minute?"

She looked up from where she'd been pretending to not see him. "Sure," she said, closing her laptop. "What's up?"

He grinned at her. "Not a lot, but I haven't really seen you much since the kitchen party and I wondered if you'd like to go for a bike ride later today? Or a walk? Or something?"

She had to laugh. "That's pretty wide open, isn't it? Sure, I guess so. Whatever. I do have a bike," she added.

He looked a bit abashed. "Actually, I knew that," he admitted. "I went past your place the other day and saw it on your car. There are some pretty good mountain biking trails around here; I'd be happy to show you."

"Were you spying on me?" she said with mock anger, while her inner voice accused her of flirting.

Declan grinned. "Not really, or maybe not exactly," he said. "But it isn't a secret that I like you and I'd like to get to know you better. So biking, yeah, something we might have in common. You can't be too mad about that, I hope."

"Nah, I'm not mad." She looked down. "I have a deadline for a project, so I have to get some productive time in this morning."

"Me, too," Declan said. "Not a project, but Russ needs me on the boat, so I'm working, too. I'll call or text you when we get off the water and finished up. If you have time then, maybe we can try a trail or two."

"Sure," Mackie agreed. They shared contacts and Declan headed to sit with the men, where Cassandra had already served his regular breakfast. As soon as he left, Cassandra took his place at the table.

"Well?" she demanded. "You guys got something going on, or what?"

Mackie gave her a stare. "Excuse me, Miss Nosy!" Cassandra had the good grace to laugh and Mackie did, too. "Not much going on here, I guess," Mackie said, "for my little social life to interest anybody."

Cassandra shook her head. "Well, I'm interested in your social life, but the rest of the town wants to know about Declan's. He's like the most eligible guy around and he's not had a girlfriend for forever."

Mackie was shocked. "And everybody knows it, right? That's why everyone keeps telling me about him. The entire town thinks they need to fix us up."

"Well, not you so much," Cassandra admitted, "but him. He's a great guy and nobody can figure out why he's still single." Mackie peeked over Cassandra's shoulder toward Declan, who was busy eating with the men, but who also appeared eager to get going and out on the water.

"Well, he's pretty cute," Mackie said. "But I don't know anything much about him."

"Doesn't matter. What matters is he seems to be interested in you, the mysterious girl from away. And do you like him?"

"Well, yeah, why not?" Mackie said. "But I just told you, I hardly know him. And I'm only here for a visit. A long, extended visit, but a visit for sure."

"Cassandra!" Sonny's voice sounded irritated. "Meals up!"

"Gotta go!" Cassandra said, sliding quickly out of the booth. "Cinnamon roll for you today? I'll be right back." She gave Mackie a silly grin and bounced off, saying, "Yeah, Sonny, right here. I'm always right here."

The fishing crowd cleared out, leaving Eric sitting over his coffee cup at a front table. Mackie reached into her bag, pulled out a book, then headed toward his table. She slipped into the seat across from him.

"Good morning," she said. He looked up from his coffee-gazing.

"Oh, look!" he said with a smile. "It's Mackenzie from Massachusetts."

She put the book on the table. "I found this in the study at the house where I am staying, at the Hamiltons'. I wondered if you knew this book."

Eric picked it up. "Oh, my, yes. Classic. *The Year of Living Dangerously*. This was the first one I read about Indonesia. Did you read it? What did you think?" His steely-blue eyes bored into hers.

"No, I haven't," she stumbled. "Should I?"

"Oh, yes," he affirmed, "at least if you're interested in different times, different people, different places. It's been a long time since I last saw it, but I think I have a copy over at Kathy's."

"Kathy?" Mackie's ears pricked.

"Yeah, where I live. At Kathy's." He looked at her then clarified, "At my daughter's house. I live over there now."

"Oh, right," Mackie said, feeling punched in the gut. Kathy. His daughter.

"I thought you were going to come play crib with me," Eric said a little querulously. "Read your books, but let's play some crib."

She nodded. "Okay, but I can't today. I have to work." She nodded back toward her laptop.

"'S'okay," he said. "You know where to find me."

IT WAS AFTER FOUR WHEN Declan and Mackie arrived at the mountain bike trail. Much as she tried, Mackie couldn't help noticing his well-muscled legs and strong arms. He easily lifted the bikes off the racks on his vehicle, while she gathered helmets, gloves, and water bottles. Murphy was enthusiastic, too. It was warm and there were hours before the sun would set. It would be a brilliant afternoon to ride. They set off along a rough road through a cut-over field, but soon enough the single track bike trail led them uphill into the woods. Mackie felt the sweat trickling down her back as she breathed a little harder. This was a real hill and the trail wasn't at all smooth. Mackie noted roots, rocks, and the occasional trickle of a stream. Some track had boardwalks traversing the wettest areas. Declan explained that they were to keep bikes out of places that could be easily eroded. Murphy bounded through the woods and then back to the trail, keeping his nose to the ground. By the time Declan and Mackie pulled up to have a drink, Murph was ready for a rest, too. He found them at a wide point in the trail and flung himself on the ground, belly flat on the cool earth, panting.

"Look at Murph," Mackie laughed. "I know just how he feels."

"Yeah, these hills and this single track can be challenging. But you seem to handle it well. Have you done a lot of mountain biking?"

Mackie shook her head. "Not a lot, but some. My ex-husband biked and I went with him sometimes."

Declan raised his eyebrows. "Oh, so there's an ex-husband." He looked at her, waiting for more.

"Yup. Are we about ready to go on?" Mackie asked.

Declan laughed. "I can take a hint. I will not ask about the ex-husband."

Mackie felt a little bad; of all the parts of her past, her divorce from Andrew was the most easily explained. "I don't mind talking about him, but it's a long story and right now we're riding. I'll tell you later, if you really want to know."

"That's good enough for me, Mackie. Thanks. And yes, if you're ready, let's get going. Murph will not be leading the way, apparently. But I bet he'll follow." They headed uphill again.

The mountain bike trail came out on a flat promontory overlooking the bay. They gazed eastward toward the water. A hint of pink lit the sky, reflected from the late day sun behind them.

"It is so beautiful," Mackie breathed. "I never really imagined that this place would be like this." They dropped their bikes and walked together toward the precipice. Declan reached for Mackie's hand and they stood at the edge watching the colors ripple on the water.

"How did I never know about this place?" Mackie wondered out loud. "It looks like something on a postcard with those dark cliffs and green forests and the colors on the water."

"I know," Declan agreed. "I didn't really appreciate it until I was away for a few years, but now I try to take time to really see where I live. I'm so glad you are seeing it, too."

Murphy came up and bumped his head against Mackie's other hand, reminding her that the dog had his priorities, dinner being primary among them. She petted him but kept gazing east, soaking in the vibrant life around them and the feeling of Declan's hand in hers. Murphy moved and barked, getting her attention.

"We probably need to start down," Declan said, noting the change in the daylight. "The sun sets really late this time of year, but it can be dark in the woods and we aren't prepared for that."

Mackie found it hard to leave the moment, but when she picked up her bike and headed back into the woods behind Declan, the technical riding absorbed her attention. When they arrived at Declan's truck, she said, "Thank you so much for taking me up there. This has been a wonderful afternoon."

Declan loaded the bikes while Mackie piled other things into the truck, calling Murphy to climb in. Declan opened his glove box and located a dog biscuit, which Murphy gratefully inhaled before crashing to sleep in the back seat.

Mackie stretched out her shoulders. "I think I know how Murphy feels," she said ruefully. "That was a lot of exercise for somebody who works online."

"Hot bath," Declan stated authoritatively. "Hot bath and a glass of wine. Do you have dinner plans?"

"Ah, whatever I can find in the fridge. As usual."

"How about this: I'll drop you off for your hot bath and come back in an hour with food. That okay with you?" Declan looked over from the steering wheel. "We both need an early night but we need to eat, too."

She nodded. He was right about the early night. Being at the diner for a five a.m. breakfast meant that most of her evenings ended before dark. "That's really nice, Declan. Thanks. It would be pretty great to not eat yogurt from the fridge tonight."

"Okay, then, it's settled. Here you go...home sweet home, and I'll be back in an hour or so with food of some sort."

Exhaustion was setting in, but Mackie was glad that her day with Declan wasn't over yet. She and Murphy headed into the house where kibble for the dog took priority over a hot bath for the human, but only for a few minutes. Soon she sank gratefully into a hot tub, nearly nodding off. But Declan was coming back. She felt a bubbling excitement in her belly. Declan at her house for the evening; that seemed to be full of possibility.

By the time Declan got back with a container of takeout Thai food, Mackie was so sleepy she could barely think about food. Murphy was flat out on the dog bed, to the point that he did not even lift his head when Declan arrived at the door.

Mackie invited him in, suddenly shy, and pointed him toward the kitchen. She pulled plates, glasses, and cutlery out while Declan found placemats and napkins for them both and opened a bottle of white wine. They sat down to a delicious-smelling meal of chicken pad Thai.

"I'm starving," Mackie acknowledged, "and the food smells amazing."

"Wine?" Declan asked, bottle poised over her glass.

"Sure," she said. "Why not?"

They ate hungrily and Mackie sipped at her wine. Declan cleared the plates to the kitchen sink while Mackie sat gratefully at the table. By the time he sat down to look at her, he shook his head. "Thanks for a great day, Mackie," he said. "I kind of hoped it wasn't really over yet, but I can tell that it is."

Mackie was embarrassed. She felt like a child needing a nap. "I'm so sorry, Declan. I had so much fun with you. I hoped we could have a long evening together. I would love to spend more time with you, but I am asleep right here with my eyes open."

He laughed again gently. "I can see that." He traced her cheek with one finger. "Well, Mackie, I think I'd best be heading home. You look knackered. And frankly, I'm not much better."

She looked up at him, bleary. "Knackered? Is that a word? It sounds like how I feel."

"Yep, take it from your local English teacher. Good night, Mackie from Massachusetts," he said lightly and bent toward her, brushing her cheek with his lips. Before she knew it, he was gone. She touched her cheek, letting her fingers linger there. It had been quite a day.

She felt the crush of disappointment as she heard the truck start up and the tires crunch out of the driveway, but soon she succumbed to sheer exhaustion and headed upstairs to her welcoming bed.

THE NEXT DAY, MACKIE headed to the fish house after eleven a.m. She carried coffee in paper cups and a couple of peanut butter cookies from the bakery in a paper bag.

She pulled the screen door open and let it slam, hard. "Hello," she called.

Eric might have been snoozing, but the slam alerted him. "Who's that? Oh, it's Miss Mackenzie!" he welcomed. "You got coffee there, don't you?"

"Yes, I do, coffee from the Sunshine, but cookies from Beth's Bakery. Maybe you don't like cookies."

He looked at her archly. "Right. Who doesn't like cookies? Have a seat. I'll get the cribbage board out."

She settled at the card table, taking tops off the coffee cups and flattening the cookie bag to set them out. Eric looked at the spread and looked at her. "Don't think I'm going to go easy on you because you brought cookies, you know," he warned. "Not too many people beat me at crib."

"Oh, talking trash already," Mackie gibed. "How do you know how I play crib? You might be feeling a little scared or something."

"Ha," he said. "Let's see who knows what they're doing around a cribbage board. You're too young to know much about this. You millennials never had to entertain yourselves; always got a tablet or something." He looked up at her. She was unimpressed.

"Still talking trash, I hear," she said calmly. "Cut for deal." Mackie was strangely calm and amused by their repartee. This she knew. This was exactly how her mother talked to her as she taught her by beating the tar out of her repeatedly. Mackie learned how to ignore the talk and watch the game. Eyes on the game and don't miss any opportunities.

As predicted, Eric beat her soundly in the first game. He chortled and wagged his eyebrows at her. "See? Not too many people beat me."

Mackie swiped up the cards to shuffle them. "Get ready," she said. "I was just warming up."

He laughed and they were at it again. As Mackie took the lead, she asked, "So, how long have you been fiddling?"

"Most of my life," he commented absently, rearranging the cards in his hand.

"And what's your favorite music to play?" she persisted.

"Oh, you know, those old tunes my grandfather played," he said, attention on his cards.

"The Irish ones? Like Turlough O'Carolan? Or old folk songs? What about the local stuff?"

He looked up at her, irritated, and then grinned. "Ah, that's a ploy, isn't it? Trying to steal the game by making me make a mistake. Ha! You'll not have the best of me. And what do you know of Turlough O'Carolan anyway?"

She looked innocent and shrugged. "Oh, my mother liked Celtic music," she said. "But don't let me distract you from being beaten at cribbage."

He pulled his eyebrows together to focus on his cards. "Frig! You're not only going to beat me, but I might get skunked. This is unacceptable."

"Frig! What kind of word is that?"

"Ah, quit friggin' around with me, Mackie. Play your cards." A smile played on his face.

An hour later, the coffee and cookies were a memory and the two of them were laughing over the outcome of their games when Russ stuck his head in the door.

"Hey, look here. It's little Miss Massachusetts! That old guy beating you at crib?" he asked, confident. Eric snorted.

Mackie's answer was brief. "Once." She looked at Eric and they laughed together.

"Yeah, once, Russ, but there will be another day. There will be another game. She's not getting away with this."

Russ grinned. "Well, who would have guessed? Eric, how are you going to show your face in town?"

"Yeah, yeah," Eric muttered. "She got lucky, that's all." But he gave her a very friendly grin. "Rematch, Miss Massachusetts. There will be a rematch."

She nodded her assent. "Sure. I'm willing to beat you again."

He shook his head. "Kids these days."

Russ was checking in. "Hey, Eric, I'm heading home now. Want a lift?"

"Yup, sure," Eric said, looking around the fish house. "I can go. Thanks for the game, Mackie," he said as he leaned on the table to stand up. He stumbled a bit, heading toward the door.

"Coming?" Russ asked Mackie. "I'm going to lock up here."

"Yes, thanks," she said and left to walk down the boardwalk to her car. "See you later," she called, waving to Eric and Russ. *A pretty good day after all*, she thought. *I spent the afternoon playing cribbage with my father. My father.*

He may not know it, but I just beat my father at cribbage. She sighed deeply, feeling happy and relaxed for the first time in ages.

Connecting

A few days later, Mackie woke late, missing her five a.m. breakfast with the locals. However, she had an eight a.m. breakfast with Murphy and that seemed just right for this day. Her muscles were still a little sore from mountain biking a couple of days ago but overall she felt pretty good. The morning with her father playing cribbage definitely had something to do with her mood, too.

She tackled her work with vigor and plowed through a pile of material she'd been stockpiling for a rainy day. It wasn't rainy, but a day to focus on her home and her work seemed like the right thing at the moment. She felt productive and ready to get work done.

By the late afternoon, she was thinking of Declan. She sent him a text.

I wasn't the most amazing hostess the other night, her message read. *Give me another chance?*

Instead of Declan, Cassandra called. "Hey, Mackie!" Cassandra was someplace noisy and so she was shouting. "Bowling? Want to come bowling with me?"

Now Mackie could place the background racket. "Not tonight, thanks, Cassandra," she shouted back. "Some other time."

"Okay, Mack. See you!"

She clicked off and wondered about herself. Why would she be willing to see Declan but not go bowling with Cassandra? *That's not being tired*, she argued with herself. *That's something else. Like you really like Declan. Right?*

I really like Cassandra, her other part pointed out calmly. *So no need to get all worked up.*

Yeah, but you know you didn't come here to meet a man, the inner voice insisted. *It doesn't matter that he is extremely cute, that he likes you, and that everyone in town wants to pair you up. It doesn't matter how great his legs look when biking, or that he knows the best places for sunsets and pad Thai. Don't get sidetracked.*

So why did I come here? Mackie asked herself, clearly feeling the inner turmoil. *He's the nicest man I have met in forever, and so what's the problem?*

The problem, Mackie, said her most precise and particular internal part, *is that you are here to connect with your father. Your parental unit who has no idea that you even exist.*

Now wait a minute, she argued back. *He certainly does know that I exist. He also knows that I can beat him at cribbage.*

Yeah, Mack, but he has no idea that you're his daughter. You're the only one in this relationship with all the information. How fair do you think that is?

Mackie got up to pour some peppermint tea. This internal dialogue was getting serious.

And speaking of fair, what about Kathy?

Ah, yes, Kathy.

The elephant in Mackie's mind. The one she had been carefully ignoring for a week while she played cribbage, found books, and biked with a cute guy. Kathy.

If Eric didn't know he had a child born in Maine, then Kathy surely didn't either. *Eric was a father to someone other than me*, Mackie thought. What kind of father was he? What kind of daughter was Kathy?

Suddenly Mackie caught her breath as another thought struck her. What kind of sister was Kathy? A light went on. Kathy was her sister.

What kind of daughter, what kind of sister, was Mackie, if she continued to hold this information a secret? What would it mean to let it out? The pressure suddenly felt intense, as if a big storm was brewing. Instead of being just a thought in her mind, Eric was a whole person. And Kathy, too, was another whole person whom Mackie had yet to meet. And the both of them were her closest living relatives.

What would happen if she told? Rejection, of course, was possible. It's what her mother had believed, after all. They might deny this truth of their family relationship, or hate it, or hate her. Maybe it was better to keep the secret. Mackie could finish her year in Stella Mare and then leave, knowing what she knew but not sharing it. This would keep her safe from rejection. It would keep her safe from the overwhelming feeling of loneliness that she felt when she lost first her husband, then her baby, and then her mother. She would not have to feel the sense of losing someone again.

For some reason, Declan came to mind. She felt a warm glow when she thought of him. But that was also dangerous. She was beginning to really like him, to think thoughts about hugging him or feeling his gentle touch on her cheek. Those thoughts were a little uncomfortable for her. She didn't want to want anyone ever again. Rejection was hard. Losing people was hard. It was better, maybe, to just not let on, so that rejection wasn't personal.

But still. Mackie shook her head. *That's the old story*, she told herself. *That's Mama's story. If I still believed that I would have stayed in Somerville. I just need to tread carefully, like Pat said. Just take my time. Let people get used to me. Maybe even Kathy.*

It was going pretty well now with Eric. Even if she didn't share the whole truth, it might be a good idea to meet Kathy. Maybe she would like Kathy, too. It could be that maybe she and Kathy could become friends. Maybe she and Kathy were alike in some ways. That thought stopped her in her tracks. A sister. She had a sister. But why on earth would Kathy be interested in her?

At this point in her ruminations, the phone buzzed. Declan was calling.

"Hey," he said warmly. "Get some sleep?"

"I feel a lot better," Mackie admitted. "Thanks for being understanding. But I'm also feeling a little ashamed, like a little kid, and I think I owe you dinner. Or something."

Her voice shook a little. Or something? What did she mean by that?

"Pizza? Do you eat pizza?"

She laughed. "Is there anyone who doesn't? Of course I do."

"Let's go get some pizza then. I can pick you up or you can meet me at Giorgio's." He gave her the address, she agreed to meet him, and they hung up.

Now what? she thought to herself. *I like him and I seem to keep pointing in his direction. But can I trust him?* She remembered how he stopped pressing her about her ex-husband when she set a limit there. Laudable. Maybe he could be an ally. She still didn't know what to do next though.

"THAT WAS DELICIOUS," Mackie sighed, patting her mouth with her napkin. "Like real Italian pizza, just like in Boston."

Declan grinned. "You'd be amazed what we have here. Don't make any assumptions."

Mackie decided to take him at his word. She had been making a lot of assumptions, some of them about Declan. She studied him as he sipped his drink, his other arm stretched across the back of the booth. She noted his calm, good-humored face, and his warm smile when he looked at her. She recalled his willingness to drop a subject when she was reticent, and his avowed interest in people in general. Here was a man who was respected and liked by the people of this town, from the old fishermen to teens and their parents. A man who had taken an interest in her, Mackie, and who had been unfailingly kind and helpful. People trusted Declan Kelly. Could she?

Maybe it was time to let him in on her mission. She took a deep breath and leaned on the table.

"So, I wonder if I can talk to you about something," she started quietly. "I've spent some time hanging around playing cribbage with Eric Johnson."

Declan looked at her curiously. "Yeah, I knew that. I kind of wondered what was the attraction? He's a good guy, but I wouldn't have thought he'd be so interesting to you."

"Yeah, well, about that." Mackie drew a breath. "You know I can beat him, right?" She grinned at Declan and he laughed.

"I had heard a rumor that the young woman from Massachusetts knew her way around a cribbage board, yes. What are you, a champion or something?"

She looked at him, becoming serious. "No, my mother taught me how to play, and since it was just us, we spent a lot of time with a cribbage board." She considered her next statement.

"You know my mother died recently," she said, looking at the table. "And that really left me with nobody. She said she had no family, and I certainly never met any of them."

"She said no family?"

"Yes, that was the story. She had no family and so I had no family. Except her, of course, but when she died that left me with nobody at all."

Mackie looked up at Declan. "I'm sorry to be taking up your time with this, Declan. I haven't talked about this. It's hard." She swallowed.

He reached across the table to cover her hands with his. "Take your time, Mackie. You can tell me whatever you want to. I'll listen."

She nodded but pulled her hands away and twisted them in her lap instead. "Yeah, so my mother's story is no family. But then it turns out that maybe I am related to Eric Johnson. So I kind of wanted to find out if that is really true. And, to be honest, whether I wanted to be related to him. He didn't impress me much at the kitchen party." She looked down at the table, absently tracing a line through the condensation from her drink.

"You didn't like his fiddling?" Declan asked, with a small smile. She looked up at him, brow furrowed. "No, okay, I see this is important. He was piss-ass drunk and pretty unpleasant, even though he somehow plays a great fiddle, regardless. So that's why you disappeared from the party. You didn't know what to make of Eric. And somehow you thought he might be your cousin, right?"

She shook her head. "The whole thing is pretty confusing to me. I am pretty sure he's the Eric Johnson I'm looking for, but he clearly isn't looking for me and never has been."

"Cousins are everywhere, Mackie. Why would a cousin be looking for you?"

She gripped the edge of the table with both hands and felt herself grow pale under his gaze.

"Mackie," Declan said carefully, "just what kind of relation is he? I thought you were looking for cousins?"

"Yeah, well, it isn't cousins," she admitted. She paused. "I, um, I think he might be my father."

"Oh." Declan leaned back. "Oh, that's something." He took a moment, pondering. "But you're not sure?"

She shook her head. "It's complicated. For a lot of reasons. I never knew anything about my father. My mother got pregnant very young, was estranged from her whole family because of it, and raised me completely on her own. She told me at first that I had no father, but when I got old enough to know that wasn't true, she told me he didn't want us. Not her and not me. But she never told me anything else about him."

"That must have been hard," Declan noted. "Is that why you never knew your grandparents, or any aunts or uncles?"

"I guess. The idea of an extended family hardly even occurred to me. I was just a kid and my mother told me that she had no family. I believed her. But now I realize that I don't even know if it's true. It turns out she wasn't completely honest with me about my father. Maybe she lied about more than that." Hot, painful tears arose. Mackie turned her face away and struggled to compose herself. Declan reached across the table to put his hand on hers.

"And your mother died," Declan stated gently, "before she could tell you more."

Mackie nodded. "She never told me anything, really. She died last winter, too young after a small and awful life. There was nobody to inform. I didn't have anyone I had to call to tell them she was gone. She didn't have anybody but me. It was just the two of us forever, except when Andrew showed up."

"Andrew? The ex-husband?"

Mackie nodded. "Mama thought he was the best thing ever. He was ten years older than me and already knew how he wanted to live his life. Mama told me to grab him, do whatever it took to keep him, so I wouldn't have to be like her. So I did. It worked for a while, as long as I was willing to fit into Andrew's life just the way he wanted me to. And I could do that for Mama, because it seemed to make her happier."

Declan's eyes were so soft and kind that Mackie couldn't bear to look at them. Abruptly, she stood up. "I didn't mean to get into so much detail. Sorry. I just wanted to tell you, tell somebody, a little about this. It's pretty much a mess. Sorry to dump on you."

"Wait! Hold on a minute, Mackie. I don't need to hear any more. That's okay. It sounds like you maybe need to find out more about our Eric Johnson. I might be able to help you do that."

"Oh? What are you thinking?" She sat back down.

"Well, you know Eric has a daughter, Kathy. She's married to my cousin, and old Eric lives at her place a little way out of town. I could introduce you to Kathy, maybe, if you wanted to do that." He looked at her intently. "Maybe that would help you figure some of this out. We could go and see her tonight, if you like."

Yes. Declan had come to the same conclusion as Mackie. She needed to get to know Kathy. Kathy, who could be her sister. Kathy, who probably also had no idea that Eric might have another child. Mackie felt herself shrink away from the idea of this interaction. At the same time, she was drawn to meeting Kathy. How else would she be able to find anything out?

"Thanks, Declan. That's probably a really good idea. But right now I don't think I can do it. I feel like just telling you this stuff, that feels like it was a lot. It's hard for me to talk about. Maybe I need to sleep some more." She smiled ruefully at him. He was very kind and being sweet, but she didn't know what she could expect from Kathy, and if she was going to be rejected again, she needed to prepare for it.

"I do have an ulterior motive," Declan confessed. "If I help you with your project, you know, trying to find your family, I'll get to spend more time with you. I like the time we spend together."

Mackie felt that excitement in her belly again. "I like it, too. I really like being with you." *And I trust you*, she thought, *or I wouldn't have told you all of this.* "But maybe it can be another night. To visit Kathy, I mean."

"Sure," he agreed easily. "You can let me know when you want to go." Mackie felt relief. He wasn't pushing her; she had been right to trust him.

He was still talking. "In the meantime, I know where to find ice cream on warm waffle cones right here in town. See, I'm giving you my winning smile to convince you that you really need dessert, after a pizza."

She laughed at his expression. But ice cream on top of pizza! That might be going too far. "Well, maybe I can go for a walk and work up an appetite."

"That's a great idea. By the time we get to the Dairy Hut you'll be ready to eat again." He was right, he did have a winning smile. She couldn't help but smile back.

"You know, Mackie, we can probably drop by to see Kathy and Jake most any evening. Eric may or may not be there. He lives in a little cabin on their property and takes his meals with the family, but only if he feels like it."

"Okay, then," she agreed, feeling better. "Some other night we'll visit but tonight we'll go for a walk that might have ice cream at the end of it."

Mackie stopped by the cash register to pay for their pizza while Declan got their jackets. They met up at the door. "Thanks for dinner," Declan said. "Hey, are you listening?"

Mackie was still preoccupied. Kathy, her probably sister Kathy, was married to Jake. How old was Kathy? What was her life like? She got to have Eric as a father. What was that like? And oh, there were so many things that Mackie wanted to know. "Do Kathy and Jake have children?" she asked. Children. She thought briefly of the baby she had lost.

"Oh, yeah, of course you'd want to know. Yes, they have three. Simon, the oldest, is off to Montreal to school, and Terence and Tate are in high school. Twins. Sixteen, I think. They go to the regional"—he grinned at her again—"you know, where I teach. It's a small community, and the kids don't mind trying to make use of family connections."

"Simon, Terence, and Tate," Mackie repeated. Older kids, almost adults. Kathy must be a lot older than Mackie. But now there were more people to consider. Maybe she had even more family. Maybe or maybe not. She wondered if she would ever know, or if it would make any difference. A lot depended on how they received surprising news. And whether she herself decided to tell them. It all felt risky.

She and Declan set out on their walk through town, questing for ice cream. She did her best to quiet her mind and pay attention to the late sunset, the emerging stars, and the man beside her. She noticed how easily they fell into step, more quickly than that first time they walked together through town. She noted the warmth in her body and her awareness of his nearness. She felt good being with Declan and, when they finished their ice cream and headed back toward the pizza shop, she was sorry the evening was ending. At the same time, she needed to get home to ponder what she had learned.

"Thanks for the pizza," Declan said again.

"Thanks for the ice cream and the walk. And for listening," Mackie returned. She reached out to shake his hand at the same time he reached both arms out to her and they bumped, awkwardly. With a giggle, Mackie switched to a high-five and he matched her, then dived in to kiss her cheek.

"Good night, Declan." She slipped into the Corolla to head up the hill where Murphy was snoring on his bed.

AS USUAL, MACKIE CURLED into herself while she processed the new information. She felt raging regret at being so open with Declan. *What was I thinking? I didn't even ask him to keep it private. How can I trust him? I lost my good sense because he is so nice and he's handsome and he seems to like me.* She felt herself shrink further into her shell, literally curling into a ball on the couch. Murphy nudged her with his wet nose.

She petted his curly head, but he was persistent. "Oh, you. I thought you were here to comfort me, but you're really looking for a treat." When he heard "treat," Murphy headed for the kitchen. Mackie reluctantly uncurled her legs and stood up. Yes, they still worked.

As she went to pull a dog treat from the tin in the kitchen, her mind went to Kathy. Kathy and her family. What were they like? What would Kathy think about her? As she moved out of her puddle of self-recrimination her curiosity about Kathy rose. What would this sister be like? Who would she look like? She must be older, but how much older? Mackie felt the fear in her belly and the warmth in her chest, along with a push-pull feeling about Kathy and Eric and all of Stella Mare. What was she doing here? She thought about leaving, right now, and the empty feeling she'd have driving back to Somerville. At least here she had a chance of finding something that might be good. Or not. But this was no longer just a hypothetical idea. These were real people, with real lives. The stakes were feeling higher and higher.

For the first time she felt her fear and her desire the same time. Could the desire to connect be stronger than the fear? Or could she do the thing she was afraid of even though she was afraid?

"Hi, Declan?"

"Oh, hi, Mackie. It's nice to hear your voice. What's up?"

"Um, I wondered if you wanted to come over later this evening. I think I owe you some more information." Mackie's voice was low.

She could hear Declan's smile. "You don't owe me anything, Mackie. You get to keep yourself to yourself and that's okay. And I can't come this evening; I already told Russ I'd help him move a trailer."

She listened closely. Was this rejection? Maybe he didn't want to hear what she had to say. Maybe he was done with her.

"Hey, Mack, you want to come help move the trailer? We can probably use some extra hands."

Mackie was shaking her head even though she knew he couldn't see her. "No, thanks, Declan. That's okay. I'm pretty sure you guys have it well under control."

"That's probably true, Mack, but I wouldn't mind seeing you," Declan offered. "I never mind seeing you."

So maybe it wasn't rejection.

"Breakfast tomorrow?" she suggested. "Are you fishing?"

"Nope, not tomorrow. So I could have breakfast at a 'civilized' hour, to quote my grandmother. She never really adapted as a fisherman's wife. She was one of those people who came from away, you know." He was laughing, and she had to giggle, too. Nobody in their right mind ate breakfast at four thirty a.m., did they? Except if you were going fishing.

"Okay, then, come on out here for breakfast," Mackie found herself saying. "I can probably make a decent enough cup of coffee. Come at eight, if you can stand having breakfast in the middle of the day like that."

He laughed. "That's like a weekend during the school year. Sounds good. I'll see you in the morning."

Declan was unavailable, but Mackie still needed to talk. She was restless, agitated, and needed some wisdom. Where could she find that in Stella Mare?

Wisdom: that might mean one of the older women she had met. Skerrit from the kitchen party, or Pat, Cassandra's mother. Yes, maybe Pat would have some time for her. Pat seemed to be a person who could keep her own counsel and she clearly had told Mackie that she would respect her privacy. Mackie sent a quick text to Cassandra, getting an immediate phone call in return.

"Why do you want to talk to my MOTHER?" Cassandra was excited and intrigued. "I've barely seen you in a couple of weeks and you want my MUM?"

Mackie felt a bit abashed. Cassandra might also be capable of keeping her own counsel, at least she said she would, but Mackie was unconvinced. But Cassandra was right. They had spent little time together. "Tell you what, Cassandra, maybe you and I can visit your mother after you get off work. How was bowling, by the way?"

Mackie was off the hook, just like that, as Cassandra began a long story about who was bowling and who said what to whom. By two thirty, she had gotten herself invited over to see Pat for an hour before Cassandra was due to arrive.

She arrived with Murphy in tow and settled into the kitchen table, again finding Pat's warm, calm presence a balm.

"Thanks so much for seeing me, Pat. I really need some wisdom from someone who is not involved in my situation. I hope that's okay with you."

Pat smiled as she poured tea. "I don't promise wisdom, but I do promise to be honest and to keep private information private. And I am glad to talk with you, Mackie."

The welcome comforted Mackie. "So I'm getting to know people here," she started. "I might be related to some. You remember I told you that when we met?"

Pat nodded. "I remember. I remember that you didn't want to talk too much about that back then. Are things different now?"

Mackie nodded gratefully. Count on a counselor to pick up the nuances.

"I think I might be closely related, as you know, to some people here, but they don't know," she confided, wondering why she still couldn't say it right out loud. "And I don't know for sure exactly, but I have wondered if it's unethical, maybe, or something like that, for me to know something that might make a difference to people and for me to just not tell them."

"Hmm," Pat murmured. "Like, is it okay to keep a secret if you're not the only person affected by the secret?"

"Yeah, something like that," Mackie agreed. "How do you decide whether to share some information that could upset people? Or maybe the information could be good? When you don't know how it will be received?"

Pat nodded over her cup of tea. "You have been thinking a lot about this, Mackie."

Mackie nodded. "A lot of thinking, but not a lot of deciding. The whole thing makes me want to run away, or hide, or spill it all and see what happens."

Pat looked thoughtful. "First, is there any danger to anyone if they don't know or if they do know? That's a kind of bottom line in ethical decision-making. Is anybody going to be hurt by knowing or by not knowing?"

Mackie looked quizzical. "You mean like hurt, like physically hurt? No, there's no danger that I can even imagine. It is just information. Suddenly to find out that you might have more relatives than you knew. That kind of information."

"Okay. Then another way to look at a question like this is what the costs are. What does it cost you to keep the secret? And what does it cost you to share it?"

Mackie pondered that. Pat waited, then added, "And for the other people involved, what are the costs for them? Can you know any of this?"

"I just don't know," Mackie admitted. "I don't know if I can even guess about this stuff. And I don't want to tell many people who are not involved if I don't tell the people who are involved. If it is a secret, it should be a secret from everyone. I'm not interested in starting rumors. The last thing I want is for Eric and Kathy to hear about the situation from somebody other than me. Does that make sense?"

Pat nodded. "Absolutely. And you don't have to tell me anything. I expect that's why you came here to talk this out."

"So the costs to people if I tell and if I don't tell. And the benefits of both. Those are what I should think about."

"And Mackie, don't forget to consider the costs and benefits to yourself while you are thinking about this. It isn't just about Eric and Kathy, but it is very much about you, too. What is it that you need and want?"

"I don't usually think that way, about what I need and want. But I will consider it." Mackie smiled up at Pat, a little shamefaced. "Do you feel like I'm using you? You were the person who felt safest to me of all the people I have met here. I hope that's okay."

Pat gave her a reassuring smile. "Yes, it's okay. And I love my daughter, but I understand why she might not be your go-to person with this sort of thing. Speaking of Cassandra, I hear her in the driveway. Are you okay?"

Mackie nodded. "I'm very okay. I still don't know what to do, but I have some other ways to think about it now. Thanks so much, Pat." She got up and gave the older woman a hug.

At the same second, Cassandra burst in the door. "Cookies? Did she give you cookies? Mum makes the best chocolate chip cookies."

Pat and Mackie looked at each other. "Nope, no cookies. Just some good advice," Mackie said.

Cassandra grinned at them both. "Excellent. So that means you didn't eat all the cookies!" She started rummaging in a cupboard and brought a container over to the table where the three women sat and laughed over tea and cookies.

IT TOOK MACKIE THREE more days before she screwed up her courage to take another step. She called Declan and asked him to introduce her to Kathy.

"Thank you for coming, Declan. I really appreciate this," Mackie said as she climbed into his truck.

"Sure. I already said we can drop by probably anytime. She's my cousin by marriage. You'll probably like her. Jake tries to farm but he's gone back into St. Stephen to work so I think Kathy does most of the farm chores and stuff. They're hardworking people. Good people."

"But you can't tell her why I want to meet her. If she doesn't know, it would be awful to find out suddenly that your father did this."

Declan's kind eyes found hers. "Did this? You mean had another child? That's a heck of a way to refer to yourself, Mackie."

Was that how she saw herself? Mackie wondered. As somebody's mistake that nobody would now want? No wonder she was having a hard time with this stuff.

"Yeah, I guess that's what I meant. Just that, if I were Kathy and I suddenly found out that my father had another daughter, it might be a bit of a shock. Especially if he and my mother were close. You know."

"We aren't going to tell anyone anything." Declan was reassuring. "I just think you might like to meet her and besides, Eric lives out there, too. Remember? I told you that."

Kathy and Jake lived in an older farmhouse just outside of town. The barn looked newer than the house. The big red building had a metal roof. It looked sturdy and comfortable for the few cattle and two sheep that Mackie saw in the adjacent pasture. The weathered shingle of the house looked like many Mackie had seen along the coast. There were a couple of older cars in the driveway and a small cabin set back away behind the house.

A tall, sturdy woman wearing jeans, boots, and a full apron came out the door onto the porch, wiping her hands on a tea towel. She had a big smile for Declan. "Look who's coming to visit!" she enthused. "So good to see you, Declan. Who is your friend?"

"This is my new friend, Mackie, Kath. She's from Massachusetts," Declan introduced her. They entered the kitchen that smelled wonderfully of yeasty bread.

"Oh, hold on," Kathy said. "I've got to check the bread." She pulled a couple of loaf pans out of the oven, dumped them out, and expertly thumped the bottoms of the loaves. Mackie watched with fascination.

"What are you doing?" she asked.

Kathy looked at Mackie over the top of her glasses. "Just checking doneness. Do they sound hollow to you?"

Mackie shrugged. "I don't know. I can't tell."

Declan pitched in. "Thump again." Declan and Kathy agreed: the loaves sounded hollow. This time Mackie could hear it, too.

"I had no idea," Mackie admitted. "You can tell if bread is done by the way it sounds. That's amazing."

Kathy smiled. Her smile looked like Eric's, though otherwise she didn't resemble him much. "It's a good day when you learn something new. I learned that from my father," she said with a smile. "The old guy was a pain in my behind, but as I get older his wisdom makes more sense." She turned the loaves upright on the racks, filled a big stoneware teapot from the whistling kettle, and pointed Declan and Mackie toward the table. "Have a seat."

Declan said, "Kathy, Mack here thinks that Eric could be a cousin or something. She's from down Boston way, looking for ancestors and relations."

"Oh, that's nice," Kathy said, with minimal interest, sweeping crumbs off the big farmhouse table, then bringing the tea to her guests. "And so where did you two meet?"

"At the restaurant. Kathy, Mackie's looking for her cousin."

Kathy gave Declan a look. "You can't blame me for getting excited when you bring a girl here, Declan. But okay, I can play along."

Kathy finally sat after putting a plate of cookies next to the teapot. She gave Mackie a close look, much like the way Eric had peered at her. Maybe it was the same look that Mackie had given to Kathy, trying to see the family resemblance to Eric. "So where exactly did you come from, Mackie?" she asked.

"I, um, I was born in Maine. But I grew up outside of Boston and I'm house-sitting here for a while," Mackie explained for what felt like the ninety-fifth time.

"Ahh, good for you, Mackie. You look like a nice girl," she crooned. "Declan, have you taken her out to the hotel for tea yet? What are the two of you doing for fun?"

"We've been mountain biking and he's been showing me around town." Mackie fed into Kathy's curiosity. "We met at the diner. Cassandra is a new friend of mine. She introduced us."

Kathy gave Declan a hard look. "Mountain biking. Ha. Do you take a girl out for a sweaty date like that?" She turned to Mackie. "Declan hasn't been out with a girl for a year. Maybe longer. It does me good to see you two together."

Declan moved uncomfortably in his chair. "Now, Kath, we don't need a history lesson. We just need to know a little about the family."

Kathy gave him a disapproving look, but then turned back to Mackie. "Cousins, you said? How is it you think we might all be cousins?"

Mackie started. The fake story suddenly got thinner. "Uh, well, my mother always said that I had relations in New Brunswick. Johnsons. So I figured probably it was cousins. Aren't we all fifteenth cousins or something, anyway?"

"So, yes, maybe, but is that all you have to go on?" Kathy asked. "That's not a lot of information. Didn't you do an internet genealogy search, or get your saliva tested, or one of those things?"

Mackie shook her head. "That probably would have made sense, but I didn't. I just heard about Stella Mare and came. When I heard about the house-sitting, I just grabbed the opportunity. I thought it would be easier to figure out when I got here."

Kathy raised her eyebrows. "Well, there's plenty of Johnsons, that's for sure. My dad, he's one, obviously. You met him? Did you ask him about this cousin thing?"

Mackie wondered how truthful she could be here. "Yes, I met him. We've been playing crib, actually. We talked a couple of times but I didn't tell him what I thought." Well, that was the truth. She wasn't telling Kathy what she thought either.

"What's keeping ya?" Kathy queried. "If you want to know something you have to ask."

"Okay, I'll ask," Mackie agreed. "Do you think Eric could be a long-lost cousin of mine?"

Kathy looked closely at her again. "You do look some like the Johnsons. Let me get some pictures to show you." She stepped out of the room and Declan grinned at Mackie and gave her a thumbs-up. Kathy returned with an old-fashioned photo album bursting at the seams, snapshots falling out of the early pages.

"Here's some pictures of Dad when he was about your age," she pointed out. Eric looked impossibly young. "And here he is with my mum. They got married young. She was right out of high school. Eric went to Maine to go to school but then he up and joined the army. The US Army. They sent him to Vietnam. He and Mum married within three months of him coming home. He never talked much about the times outside of here. I think it was hard on my parents."

"Is your mum still living?" Mackie asked in a whisper. What if her father had been married when she was conceived? Could that explain his absence from her life?

"Oh, no, Mum died in 2000. She and Dad divorced way long before that though. I was only a baby. He wasn't really able to be a dad after Vietnam and all. Mum married my stepdad when I was four. I have three siblings, half siblings, I guess. That turned out to be a good thing!"

"Did you spend much time with Eric when you were growing up?" Mackie asked.

There was a flicker of anger in Kathy's face. "Not so you'd notice. My stepdad was a good thing for me. My own dad wasn't really able. He wasn't bad, he was just…absent." She looked pensive.

Mackie was thinking hard. "So you have siblings, but they're not Johnsons? You're Eric's child, but they aren't?"

"Yes, that's right," Kathy agreed. "Eric and Mum split up when I was tiny; I'm the oldest of four, but I'm Eric's biological child and my sibs are not."

"You weren't close when you were a kid?" Mackie was focused on Eric as a father.

Kathy shook her head. "I pretty much hated him for a long time, to be honest. I felt like he left me. Like he didn't care about me."

Declan had been listening intently. "But Kath, why do you have him here now? He's not an easy guy and you didn't really have much of a relationship when you were a kid. Why do you let him live here?"

She gazed at him and her face softened. "Oh, Declan, he's my father. I may have hated him when I was a kid, but I also didn't know what he was trying to deal with. I think Vietnam kind of ruined him and then he has never managed to stop drinking, but he's not a bad person. He wasn't much of a father to me, but he's still my dad and he needs me now. What kind of person would I be to abandon him in his old age and sick as he is?"

Declan shook his head. "I respect that, Kath, and I hope if I have children they would be so good to me."

Kathy smiled slightly. "Declan, if you have children, you'll be a very fine father. No worries about your children being on your side when you're old and ugly!" They laughed and all three of them turned as the kitchen door opened. Eric stumbled in.

"Oh, hey, Dad," Kathy breezed. "Here's Declan and Mackie, come to see you."

"See me?" Eric slurred. "Hey, Declan, pretty girl you got there."

"Dad! Mackie wants to talk to you."

His eyes struggled to focus on the trio at the harvest table. "Oh, it's you! The little card sharp from Massachusetts," he mumbled.

"Yeah, it's me," Mackie agreed, gulping. "How are you, Eric? Ready for a rematch?" Breezy, that was the ticket. That was how to pretend your heart was not about to crash through your chest wall.

"Not right now," Eric mumbled, waving a vague hand as he stumbled through the door to the living room.

"Kathy, honey, bring me a drink, will ya?" He landed on the couch. His voice grew demanding. "Kathy! I said a drink!"

"Not happening, Dad," called Kathy calmly. "You go to sleep. You'll feel better later."

Mackie stole a glance at Declan, who looked sympathetically at her. She felt a vast hollow in her chest and was aware that she was about two seconds away from crying. Declan stood up and grabbed their jackets.

Kathy looked at them. "I think your conversation will have to be another time. I'm sorry about that, Mackie."

Declan spoke. "Thanks for the tea, Kath, and the talk," he said. "We'll be in touch."

"Yes, thank you," Mackie murmured, and the two slipped out the kitchen door.

"I'm so sorry, Mack," Declan started.

Mackie shook her head hard. No. Not one word, please. She could not hold it together if she felt his sympathy. "I just need to go home."

MACKIE RETREATED BACK to her home-for-now, throwing herself into work and spending a lot of time hugging Murphy. Unlike before, though, she was not lost in her anguish. She was thinking. What was the next step?

To her surprise, people showed up. Cassandra called her. Declan dropped by with coffee on the second day. Pat sent her a package of chocolate chip cookies via Cassandra. When Mack took Murphy up the hill one day, she ran into Skerrit and Dee. They invited her over to see their collection of paintings made by local artists.

This Eric Johnson. What to make of him? Drunken Eric frightened Mackie, but fiddling, card-playing, book-reading Eric was someone she wanted to know better. She knew he drank all the time, even while they played cards, but he was not always inebriated. She thought possibly she could like him just fine, at least sometimes.

More important than what she liked, though, was the truth. Maybe Eric needed to know the truth. For sure, it was something that Kathy would want to know. At least Mackie thought so now that they had met and she'd heard Kathy's experience growing up. But she still didn't know what to do or how to do it.

What are the costs? What are the benefits? What do I really need and want? These were the questions her talk with Pat raised for her and she thought hard about all of them.

By the end of the third day, she had settled a few things. *I only know what is in my own mind*, she thought. *I can't mind-read other people, so I really can't tell what knowing or not knowing costs anyone else. I do know that keeping this secret is costing me a lot of time, energy, and worry. And I also know what I need. What I need is to know who I am and where I come from, and while I know the Sarah and Somerville part, I don't know the rest. And what I want is the truth, no matter the cost.*

Four days after her visit with Kathy, Mackie returned to her schedule and was in her booth at the diner early. Russ, Jimmy, and the guys seemed happy to greet her. Eric was there, too. He called out to her.

"Hey, Mackenzie from Massachusetts!" She heard his voice over the general din. "Where you been? I'm waiting for my rematch, you know."

She got up and headed toward the front of the restaurant. There was her father in the gathering of fishers. The last time she'd seen him he had been passing out on Kathy's couch.

"Hi," she said, approaching his table, her calm voice belying her internal state. "Are you sure you're ready for a rematch?" she teased. She still felt watchful, but it was not even six a.m. Eric most likely was stone-cold sober at this point.

"Bah!" he puffed. "I can likely beat you with my hands tied behind my back and playing cards with my teeth, you."

Mackie had to laugh. "Oh, you think so. Well, that didn't happen before, now, did it?"

"You just don't forget that you have to give me a chance to redeem myself," Eric stated, turning back to his coffee. "Come by. We'll play cards."

"Right." Mackie nodded. "What kind of deal is this? You invite me to come by, prepared to be skunked, and I have to even bring the coffee. I'm not sure that's such a great deal."

Eric's eyes crinkled with a grin. "Come on over anyway, Mackenzie."

Russ, sitting across from Eric, snickered. "It gives him something to do, Mackie, talking trash like that. My money's on you."

Mackie gave Russ a grateful smile and slid back toward her favorite booth. It felt good to be welcomed. It was almost as if she belonged.

THE NEXT DAY, MACKIE got ready to visit Eric. She felt trepidation and something else: determination. She took care of Murph and sent him off for his late-morning nap. She stopped at the little desk in the kitchen and picked up her manila envelope.

The medallion necklace fell into her hand. Her fingers closed around its familiar shape and she felt it warming in her palm. Without thinking too much, she slipped it over her head and tucked it inside her T-shirt. She put the snapshot into the back pocket of her jeans, grabbed her phone and wallet, then headed out the door.

Parking at the dock, she backed out of the Corolla with coffee in both hands, toed the car door shut, then headed toward the fish house. The tide had turned a couple of hours before, and the fishing boats were all out of sight. The harbor was quiet, except for a couple of sailboats preparing to head to open water. The sea air was crisp, but even this early Mackie could tell it was going to be a very warm day. She listened for a moment to the gulls squabbling over fish parts, to the sound of work happening in the big fish market and to the lap of little wavelets against the rocks and pier.

This is the day. Today I am going to talk to my father. Her stomach cramped as she thought those words. But there was no turning back. Determination.

Mackie took a deep breath, exhaled sharply, and turned her attention to the screen door of the fish house where Eric presumably waited. Then she walked as resolutely as she could toward her future.

Known and Unknown

Eric was there, but instead of sitting in his usual corner, carving or reading or playing solitaire, he was pacing, staring at his phone.

"Hi," said Mackie, mildly, backing in through the screen door and letting it slam per protocol.

Eric startled at her voice. "Oh, hey, Mackenzie. How you doing?" He barely glanced at her and continued his pacing around the small room.

"I'm good," Mackie said, putting the coffee on the table and looking at him curiously. "How are you?"

"Me? I'm fine, fine." He shook his head hard. He slipped the phone into his pocket and headed for the card table. "Never better," Eric stated firmly. "You here for the rematch?"

"Maybe," Mackie prevaricated. "Mostly just dropping by to see you. I need somebody to have coffee with me."

Eric looked at her. "Yeah, right. That good-looking Declan Kelly must be busy somewhere else if you want to have coffee with an old guy like me. I think you're scared of a rematch." His words were light, but his frown was not. He pulled his phone out again and glanced at it, settling his glasses firmly. Then he put it away and picked up his coffee. "Cribbage?" he asked.

Mackie didn't know how much to pry and she also was bringing a big agenda of her own today. The rematch could wait. She wanted to talk to Eric.

"I really, uh, really just wanted to talk to you." She tried to ignore her pounding heart. "Do you remember I saw you at Kathy's last week?"

Eric, puzzled, shook his head. "I don't remember a lot about last week, girl. Did I see you there?"

"Yes, you did," Mackie said firmly. "You didn't seem very well, but we saw each other. Declan was there, too."

"Declan's a good boy," Eric said mildly. "He's kin to Jake, you know. Kathy and Jake been married a long time."

"I asked Declan to take me out to meet Kathy. The reason is that I kind of wonder if we might be related," Mackie offered.

Eric's steel-blue gaze sharpened. "I remember now, when you first came here, you were looking for cousins. Cousins, you were looking for cousins. There was a lot of cross-border movement before nine-eleven, and New England is full of Canadians and New Brunswick full of New Englanders. You think you might be cousins to Kathy? On her mother's side?"

"Well, maybe not exactly cousins. But relations of some sort and not just to Kathy. To you, too," Mackie said very quietly. She pulled the snapshot out of her jeans pocket and laid it on the table with a shaking hand.

Folding her hands into her lap, she kept her eyes on the picture. There it sat. This faded color shot of two people, a very young woman and a man over forty, was the link that connected her to Eric, or at least one of the links. The girl had that eighties poufy hair, a big pink sweatshirt, and artfully bleached jeans. The man wore a plain T-shirt and ball cap. The girl had turned her face up to his and Mackie could see adoration in that girl's eyes. The man in the picture looked straight at the camera as if he owned the world, his arm around the pink sweatshirt. Mackie had spent so many hours staring at this picture it was emblazoned it on her memory. Squinting, she saw the leather thong around the man's neck and could nearly trace the shape of the medallion under his Bar Harbor souvenir T-shirt. Or perhaps that was her imagination. Suddenly the snapshot looked unfamiliar, new, as if she were seeing through other eyes. Her hand involuntarily stole to her own shirtfront, and she touched the medallion. Yes, it was real. And it was still there. She peeked at Eric.

"Where did you get this picture?" Eric demanded. "I know that girl. She's your cousin? I knew her."

Mackie shook her head. "No, she's not my cousin."

He peered at the picture, eyebrows knitted together. "That's me, isn't it? Hey, that's me." He looked hard at Mackie. "Really, girl, where did you get this picture? This is me, probably a million years ago. And a girl I knew, Linda something. She was a waitress for the summer in Bar Harbor."

She was silent, except for the pounding in her chest.

"Mackenzie."

She could barely breathe, let alone answer him.

"Mackenzie from Massachusetts, I asked you, where did you get this picture of me and Linda?" His voice was gruff and loud.

Mackie's voice came out small, unfamiliar. "That's not Linda. Her name was Sarah Brown. She was my mother."

His gaze on the picture softened a bit. "Sarah Brown, that's not right. That's Linda. I remember little Linda. We had a great summer back then."

His gaze turned to Mackie and sharpened again. "Did you say she was your mother? Was?"

Tears stung Mackie's eyes and she swallowed hard. *Don't make me say it*, she thought. "Yes. She was. Remember, I told you that Mama died last year. In December, to be precise."

"Oh, Mackenzie, I'd forgotten. That's too bad. And you said you didn't know your father, either. And your mother was Linda. Imagine that." The gruffness was gone. He picked up the picture and looked at it again. "Poor little Linda. But you called her Sarah."

"Yes. As far as I ever knew she was Sarah. Sarah Brown. Maybe she changed her name. Maybe she had a good reason," Mackie pondered. *Like she was pregnant and unmarried and scared to death,* her inner dialogue prompted.

"So you knew my mother, Eric." *Knew in the biblical sense,* Mackie's inner voice jibed. *Am I going to have to draw the connection for him? Isn't he going to get it?*

"She never said anything about being cousins though," Eric said. "Where did you get the idea that we were cousins?"

"Relatives. Relatives, Eric. Maybe not cousins." *For Pete's sake! He thinks he was related to Mama and Mama is related to me. He's just not getting it.*

She sighed a giant sigh. *Don't make me say it, don't make me say it.*

Eric's phone buzzed right then, and he pulled it out to look again at the screen. He shook his head and his eyes narrowed as he slipped it back into his pocket. Mackie suddenly felt afraid in a different way. Not afraid of Eric, but afraid of losing this moment and of never having the courage to come to this point again.

She pulled the medallion out from under her T-shirt. She held it out toward him, then slipped it over her head and dropped it into his hand.

"I have this, too, Eric," she said clearly. "And I am thirty-one years old. My birthday is April 16. I was born in 1986. April 1986."

Do I have to draw you a picture? she thought. *Please say something.*

He looked at the medallion in his hand. He slowly slid his fingers over the surface, touching the raised image and then flipping it over to stroke the engraving. She knew what he was seeing and touching. Bar Harbor, 1985. May love last forever.

Then he picked up the photo, looking once again at the happy couple in the picture. His phone buzzed insistently in his pocket but he ignored it, looking back and forth between the medallion and the snapshot.

A TALISMAN OF HOME

Very slowly, Eric shook his head. "No," he breathed. "No, no, no," he repeated, his voice increasing in volume and agitation. He looked up at Mackie and there was fire and ice in his steel-blue eyes.

"No. You will not tell me this, Mackenzie. I have done some terrible things in my life, but I did NOT leave that little girl with a baby. NO!" He flung the medallion and photo onto the table. "You get right out of here, you. Don't you come in here telling me lies!"

Mackie, terrified, scooped up her items and got out of her chair at the same time. Eric stood up on the far side of the table. His face was red and his rage palpable.

"Get out! You get OUT of here!" He flipped the card table, coffee and all, and headed toward Mackie. She backed toward the door and, as soon as she was clear, she ran to the Corolla, pulling keys out of her pocket as she went. Her hands shook as she put the key in the ignition. What had just happened? She backed out with a swirl of gravel.

MACKIE HEADED STRAIGHT home, gathered Murphy, her laptop, her coziest sweater, and drove the Corolla away from Stella Mare and toward the border. Within the hour she arrived in St. Stephen. She parked the car near a little park overlooking the St. Croix river, pulled a leash from the glove compartment, and got out with Murphy. She needed to move.

They walked along the riverfront trail. She pounded the pavement so fast and hard that Murphy had trouble keeping up. She was barely aware of the tears streaking her face. Finally, her pace slowed enough so she could take a deep breath. She wiped her face with her sleeve and bent down to give Murphy a scratch under his chin. "Sorry, buddy," she told him. "I really needed to burn off something there."

Mackie was acutely aware that over there, just across the water, was Maine. Somewhere over there, a few hours' drive, was the place that she thought of as "home." But was it really home? When she thought about home, it brought to mind people, family. Home meant who you were with, not necessarily where you were.

This had been the crux of the trouble with Andrew. Andrew didn't care about making a home and had not wanted to make a family. He even sent back a dog that Mackie had once tried to adopt.

Now Eric had made it perfectly clear that she had no claim on him as family. He might have been okay with cousins, but there was no way that he was going to accept her as a part of his actual family. Mackie felt the sharp pain of rejection again, deep in her belly. She sat on a trailside bench and bent over with the cramping feeling. Murphy rested his muzzle on her knee.

She petted him, grateful for his stable company. "Oh, Murphy," she murmured, "you still want me, right?" Murphy whined a little in response. "Woman's best friend." Mackie could smile slightly at her thought.

She looked up again across the river and across the invisible international border. *I want to go HOME,* she thought, *but I have no idea where that is. I'm American, so I guess the US is home, but where? I grew up in Somerville, but Mama is from somewhere in Maine and my apparent father is from here...even if he refuses to claim me. Do I want to fight him on this? DNA and all that? What would be the point?*

That would show him, her inner voice stated. *That would show him the truth! He couldn't hide from it anymore.*

Yeah, show him what? That he's a worse guy than he already thinks he is? Mackie questioned internally.

Well, yes. He is a worse guy. Didn't he abandon your mother and you? The pain in her belly intensified. Rejected, over and over. Her mother and her, rejected.

The inner voice weighed in again. *Remember what you learned about Sarah. Remember that she rejected before she could BE rejected. Remember that's how you lost out on any family at all. She assumed the worst and that's exactly what she got. And she blamed it all on everyone else who never got a chance to decide for themselves.*

Well, now he's got a chance to decide, doesn't he? And he decided. He decided to rage at me and turn that table over and scream at me to get out. That's rejection. You don't need an advanced degree to see that as rejection.

Yeah. True. But what was he rejecting? Was it a rejection of you, Mackenzie Brown? Or was he rejecting that new picture of himself as a terrible person who could abandon a nineteen-year-old pregnant girl?

I hate it when you make sense, Mackie groused at the rational part of herself. *I want to be wronged here. I fell into my mother's story of being wronged for almost my entire life. Letting Andrew leave without trying to save our marriage was the first thing I ever did on my own. That decision allowed me to stop being controlled by other people. Yet I still felt wronged: what was so terrible about wanting a family? And now I want to feel wronged by Eric. He didn't need to scream at me and toss a table at me. I shocked him for sure, but his reaction was over the top.*

But maybe I'm not wronged. Maybe he's just shocked by the news. So maybe I don't have to take it so personally.

She was breathing easier now and the cramp in her belly was gone. Murphy noticed a shift in her mood and got up, ready to take some action.

"Okay, Murph," she said. "I hear they've got some good chocolate in this town. We can find it." They were heading back down the trail toward the parking lot when a text came from Declan. Kathy had asked for her number and he'd given it.

Mackie felt an upswing of trepidation. What could Kathy want? Mackie could guess. After all, a few hours ago Kathy's father was throwing tables at Mackie. Kathy probably wanted to tell her off, too.

Or worse. Maybe Kathy thought Mackie should have warned her that Eric was on the warpath. There was no way out of this. Frig. That's what the locals said when things were too much. Mackie liked it. Oh, frig.

Just then her phone rang. She didn't recognize the number, but she could bet it was Kathy. Mackie felt exhausted. "I'm not ready for another one," she told Murphy, who blithely ignored her. "Not right now." Soon there was a signal to show a new voice mail. Mackie ignored that, too, and kept walking.

She put Murph in the car and found a small diner where she ordered coffee and something that looked deliciously chocolatey. She sat at a small table outside, phone upside down next to her drink. She sipped at the creamy coffee and picked at her treat but could barely taste it. *Go home, go home, go home*, played a drumbeat in her mind. *You got what you came for. Just go home.*

But where was home? Mackie shook her head to clear it. She needed to talk to somebody about this; otherwise she was just making herself crazy. She called Declan.

When he picked up, she skipped the preliminaries. "I told him, at least I sort of told him," she said rapidly into her phone. "And he threw me out and made a mess of the fish house. And I don't know what to do. I think I'm going to leave tonight, maybe, just get out. Oh, Declan, he was so mad."

She suddenly felt her own collapse into tears as she said the words. She picked up her coffee and walked away from the table, phone to her ear. Hopefully nobody noticed the woman crying over her chocolate dessert.

"Yeah, Mackie, I know," came Declan's warm, calm voice.

"What? What do you know? Did you hear already that he threw me out? Is everybody talking about it? About me?"

Declan was soothing. "Well, Kathy said Eric was upset about something, so I guessed maybe you'd had your talk. He'll calm down. I think that it's going to be okay."

"Okay? What could be okay? He hates me, Declan. I showed up and ruined his life right there. Everything is falling apart."

Declan was quiet for a moment. "Mackie? You still there?"

She nodded, then remembered he couldn't see her. "Yes, I'm here. I really just don't know what to do next. I feel terrible for about a dozen reasons. I'm kind of afraid to show up in Stella Mare, like I'll be persona non grata or something. The town protects Eric quite a bit."

"Mackie, you are not a threat to Eric or to anyone in town," Declan stated firmly. "People get upset. People get over it. Learning something you didn't know can flip your world."

Mackie listened. "Yeah. My world was pretty much flipped when I found out that Eric maybe didn't even know he had a kid. Or at least didn't know he had this kid, me. It was like my entire life with my mother was based on a big fat lie."

"And how long was it before you could really understand it?"

Mackie considered. "Well, I don't think I really understand it yet, but it was a few weeks before I could even start to imagine trying to find Eric. I wasn't sure I wanted to try, and I wasn't sure even after I arrived and met him. He's not my idealized image of the daddy I thought I was missing when I was fourteen."

Declan gave a short laugh. "Yeah, I bet. But you stayed even when it turned out that he's a regular guy with a lot of baggage. You decided to follow it through."

She let those words sink in. Yes, she had decided to follow it through. It could have been a mistake.

"It was really only last week when I decided that a real live father, baggage and all, was better than an imaginary father who rejected me. But now I got to be loudly, significantly, rejected. So tell me, did I make the right decision?" She leaned against the Corolla, petting Murphy through the partially opened window.

"I'm not the one to answer that," came Declan's response. "But I do know this: I don't want you to leave. I really like you, and I like that everyone trying to shove us together doesn't put you off, and that you have stuck to your plan even though you've had big upsets and disappointments. So as your friend who wants you to succeed, I don't want you to leave. And as a man who really likes you, a lot more than I will admit to myself, I really do not want you to leave. I would miss you. Like a lot. So maybe you can take that into account while you're making your decisions."

The words sat between them as Mackie tried to grasp them. He was right, perhaps, that her task was still incomplete. Besides, she still had a house-sitting commitment to honor. But more than that, it sounded like Declan wanted her to stay because he liked her just for herself. He wanted her to stay because he wanted her. Yes, that. What was that feeling? This feeling of being wanted was lovely. It was the opposite of rejection, for sure.

"I'm going to tell you what to do, Mackie, right now. Or, at least what I think you should do," he amended. "Call Kathy. It can't be worse than what happened this morning and maybe it will help."

Mackie shook her head again. No way. She wasn't going to do that. "I don't know if I can do that, Declan. But because you suggested it, I will consider it. Right now I'm out of town and I might stay that way for a while. It feels safer to be away from Stella Mare. But I can't tell you how much better I feel. Thank you for this talk. Maybe absolutely everything hasn't gone to pieces. Yet."

She clicked the phone off and looked at it in her hand. Call Kathy? No. She slipped the phone into a pocket and got into the car. Soon she and Murphy were on the road away from the border. She wasn't ready to leave the province yet. Not ready to give up on everything she was working on. Maybe tomorrow, but not today.

THE NOTIFICATION SAT there on her phone, practically calling out her name.

Mackie had spent the rest of the day away from Stella Mare. She took herself out for a fried seafood basket at Ossie's Lunch, late in the afternoon, and wandered the roads up to Black's Harbor, watching the ferries coming in and heading out toward Grand Manan, yet another place she'd not yet visited. As a distraction, she looked up hiking trails on the island on her phone, but the voice mail notification mocked her.

She and Murphy finally headed back to Stella Mare under cover of dusk. Mackie would have preferred full dark, but the sunset was so late this time of year that wasn't possible, at least not with her need for sleep. But she crept in through back streets, avoiding the main street, glad that her dusty Corolla was unlikely to garner any attention. She knew it was crazy, but she felt like everyone was looking at her. *Look! There's that crazy girl from Massachusetts who thinks she's Eric's daughter. What a wacko!*

Mackie shook her head. This was crazy, letting her own mind dictate what other people might be thinking. And about her of all things. Other people had their own stuff to think about, didn't they? Still, she felt better when she'd cleared her stuff from the car and she and Murphy headed indoors for the night. Murphy took his time to water the garden, but Mackie called him in sooner than he liked. When she clicked the front door locked after he wagged in, Mackie felt a sense of relief.

But then she had to face that voice mail notification. Mackie made a cup of chamomile tea and sat down on the comfy couch. The phone sat on the coffee table. When she touched it, the notification leaped out at her again.

How much damage could a voice mail do? Surely it would be okay to listen to what Kathy said. The worst thing might be to tell Mackie off and Mackie noted that she'd already been told off by a master that morning. How much worse could it be? And after she listened, then maybe, maybe, she might be able to sleep.

Quickly, before she could change her mind again, she grabbed the phone and tapped the buttons. She put it on speaker.

There was Kathy's voice. Mackie could imagine Kathy in her kitchen, wearing her boots and jeans and apron, holding the phone to her ear.

"Mackenzie," Kathy said firmly. Mackie could hear background noise, shouting and the sounds of furniture moving. "Declan gave me your number. Dad just got home, ranting and raving about you and somebody named Sarah. He's pretty upset and honestly, I don't think he's even drunk, but he says he told you off and that he's not to blame and a bunch of stuff like that. I just wanted to check in and make sure you're okay. He rarely gets that agitated with people, but I know he can be scary when he's mad. He had some bad news from his doc today, too. So please, please call me so I know you're okay and so I can let him know, too. When he comes to himself, he's going to feel pretty bad that he was mean to you."

Mackie clicked off the phone after saving the message. Why should she care how *he* was feeling? He was the one who went off on her. Mackie felt some strength from having reality on her side, for once. At least Kathy didn't also ream her out, although she might when she found out the real situation. Mackie turned her phone on again and sent a brief text to Kathy's number. *I'm fine. Thanks for thinking of me.*

There. Now Kathy, at least, could sleep. Eric no doubt was sleeping like a baby, almost certainly being liquored up. Mackie didn't really know much about being liquored up, but it sounded pretty harsh and she figured it probably made you sleep. She knew if she drank over two glasses of wine, sleep was happening.

Maybe wine, maybe tonight? Ugh, no. Chamomile tea was really more her style. Especially now that she knew that her father had a drinking problem, she didn't want to go that route.

Her phone buzzed. Kathy, return text. Oh, frig. That word was getting useful.

Dad just told me something interesting. Since you're up, can I drop by?

No, no, no! thought Mackie. *No.*

A TALISMAN OF HOME

I'm exhausted, she replied.

A pause. Then a reply buzzed in. *I bet you are; sounds like it was a hard day. Can we meet for breakfast? I want to see you in person.*

Mackie shook her head. This felt like a runaway train. Well, she started something and so she needed to see it through.

Okay, sure, she typed. *Tell me where and when.* She stopped before hitting send. She backed up the cursor and wrote, *Seven a.m. at the Sunshine Diner.* She might as well take charge. She clicked send.

Kathy agreed instantly and said good-night. Mackie turned her phone off and sat back on the couch to sip at her tea. Now what? Ten hours until breakfast. Another sleepless night in Stella Mare? She should be used to this by now.

When daylight crept loudly through the window at four forty-five, Mackie had been asleep for about four hours. That was four more than she had expected, though, so she felt good for a moment. Then she remembered in a couple of hours she'd be talking to Kathy. But about what? Could she tell Kathy what she thought was true, even though Eric denied it? Who did this story belong to, really?

Groaning, she put feet on the floor and headed downstairs to boil water for tea and let Murphy have his first outing of the day. Before the kettle boiled, the dog was back, looking for a treat and ready to start his first morning nap.

Mackie glared at him as he settled down on the kitchen dog bed. "Yeah, you can just go back to sleep," she said irritably. "Some of us aren't so carefree." She took her cup to the comfy couch, leaving Murph snoring on his own. Mackie wouldn't mind sleeping on the dog bed if it meant a few more hours of sleep. As it was, her mind was already racing. She felt the worry lines showing up on her forehead.

When the time came, she felt a little more ready. Well, she felt hungry, and that was an improvement over her stomach being full of anxious cramps. She headed down the hill toward the diner. She hoped it was late enough to miss the fishing crowd. As luck and the tide would have it, Russ and Jimmy were just leaving as she arrived. She got a wide smile and greeting from Russ. Okay, so maybe there was one person in town who didn't hate her. Yet.

She looked around for Kathy but found nobody else was in the diner. Mackie started to head to her usual booth, but then picked a table closer to the counter. Cassandra would no doubt want to know everything that went on, so Mackie figured she'd give her a front-row seat. After today, Mackie would be only a memory in Stella Mare, if that.

Mackie heard the door open and willed herself to not look up. Kathy swept in and over to the table, pulled out a chair, and sat. The two women looked at each other. Mackie looked at Kathy's eyes so like Eric's. Steel-blue, they were, but warmer, somehow, than her father's. Kathy had long, thick hair, much like Mackie's, even though Kathy's had some small streaks of gray. She saw similarities in their chins, and even how they sat at the table, leaning forward. Mackie wasn't sure she wanted to see all of this. She pulled back and away, leaning against her chair and folding her arms.

"Your mum's eyes were brown," Kathy said.

Mackie started in surprise. This was unexpected. "Yes, they were. How did you know?"

Kathy shook her head. "Remembering my high school biology, looking at your deep brown eyes. Brown eyes are dominant. Those are not Johnson eyes."

"No, you're right, they're from my mother. Her name was Brown, too, so that's maybe even a little funny. If any of this is funny," Mackie stated ruefully.

Kathy smiled. "It is true, though, isn't it? We're sisters. You are my sister."

"Half," Mackie corrected.

"Sure, half," Kathy agreed. "All of my sibs are half. I just didn't know that there was one on Dad's side. I'm not unhappy about this, Mackie."

"You're not?" Mackie was astonished. "Isn't it a shock?"

A TALISMAN OF HOME

Kathy gave a small laugh. "Surprise, yes, but not a shock. Dad was off doing who knows what for most of my life. He sort of kept in touch, but I didn't count on him for much. I think he's been trying to make up for that a little these last few years. He's got a lot of problems. He came with some of them and some he got along the way, but he's been trying a lot harder to be part of the family lately."

"I guess I threw that off," Mackie said in a tiny voice. Kathy burst out laughing.

"You know what, Mack? Dad did some pretty bad stuff in his life. He did. He's been trying to own up to his shortcomings. I think he sees his mortality, maybe, and he's been trying to make up for the past. Finding out that he had a child he didn't know about is a bit of reality. You didn't make this happen. It is a truth that he needed to learn."

Kathy's tone shifted, becoming gentler. "But honestly, I don't think he ever knew about you. He wasn't around to take part in raising me, that's for sure, but I don't think it was because of him not wanting me. And while he missed out with you, obviously, I don't think it was on purpose. He was freaking out about you thinking he'd abandoned you. He and I spent years fighting over what that means."

Mackie looked up. "And? What did you come up with?"

"Well, I suspect everyone has to do this work for themselves, but for me, I decided that there is a difference between willful abandonment and being left because being with the parent might be more damaging than being without him."

"What do you mean? Eric was damaging?"

"Likely to be, I think. I know he hit my mother more than once. I imagine that a toddler or a smart-mouth teenager would have gotten the same. Plus, he was utterly unreliable; drinking and untreated mental illness will do that to a person. Mum told me little bits. He spent wildly, including expensive presents for her and me. But no money for rent. He worked hard, but only when he worked. He had a degree but could never find work that allowed him to take days off when he was on a bender, or he flew off the handle at customers, or whatever. The stories she told would curl your hair. He's so much better now. So much better."

"You're saying that it was out of love that he left you? Really?"

Kathy grimaced. "Well, that sounds very poetic and nice, but no. I think in hindsight it was for the best for me and everyone around him he didn't stick with Mum and try to raise a family. But I don't think he could see his behavior as a decision. Maybe I've just forgiven him and appreciate that I got to have my mother and stepdad and my brother and sisters."

Mackie listened and nodded. If Eric had been as Kathy said, then maybe she, too, was better off not having known him. But no. He could have helped her mother with child support at least. Sarah had grown thin and old before her time, working multiple jobs to keep the two of them in food, clothes, and an apartment. But then, if he really didn't know about her, he couldn't have done anything.

"I know he didn't know about me," she confirmed to Kathy. "My mother was too afraid or too ashamed or too something to let him know. But I wished for a father my whole life. I wished for someone to make my mother's life, I don't know, better."

"It must have been hard."

"Yeah, all of it. And she died, you know, just last December."

Kathy shook her head. "No, I didn't know. Dad just gave me the outlines. I'm so sorry you lost her, Mackie."

"Yeah, me, too. But when I discovered who my father was, then I had a mission. I could maybe find him. Maybe he wouldn't hate me, right away. So I came."

Kathy appraised her. "That took guts, Mackie. You took a great big leap into the unknown."

"Yes and look what happened. I got thrown out of the fish house."

"I'm pretty sure he regrets that, Mackie," Kathy offered.

"How mad is he?"

Kathy wagged her head. "Well, it's a little hard to say. He got pretty plastered last night, and I haven't seen him this morning. I don't think he's mad at you, actually, though that might be hard to believe after what you went through yesterday. I think he knows that he overreacted. The news took him by surprise."

Mackie felt bad. "I didn't know how to say it," she confessed. "When I got here, I didn't know how to say I was looking for my father, of all people, and I really didn't know if it was true that he didn't know about me. And then I found out about you, and that meant you didn't know about me either. It has been very confusing."

"Secrets complicate families. But every family has them."

"Yes, apparently," Mackie agreed. "At some point I think I'll be glad that this one is out in the open. But right now, I'm still not certain. But I do know that I'm hungry. How about you? Coffee and cinnamon roll?" Kathy nodded, and Mackie waved to Cassandra, who had been waiting for the signal.

"Before we eat, Mackie, I want to tell you something," Kathy said. "I liked you right away and thought you'd be a great addition to the family. Mostly I figured it would come through Declan, but now I see it differently. I am very glad that you are my sister. You are family, regardless of Eric." She reached out toward Mackie.

Mackie swallowed hard and gratefully returned the hug. Napkins to damp eyes, they turned their attention to breakfast, explaining to Cassandra, who sat with them and raptly listened to every word.

LATER THAT AFTERNOON, Mackie sat at her kitchen table and tried to catch up on work. Thank goodness for working ahead, so maybe her clients wouldn't notice a little slippage. Or so she hoped. It was almost impossible to get her mind under control. She loved her work, but right now work was not the top thing on her mind.

She gently closed her laptop and got up for another cup of tea. Paper and pen, that's what she needed to think. Paper and something to write with, the old-fashioned way. She scrabbled around and found a set of colored felt pens and a sketch pad, and took that and her tea to the front porch.

Okay. Her good intentions took her this far, but she drew a line down the page and then was off into musing once again. *Oh, Mama. What would you do?*

Mackie gave it a moment and then tried to shrug it off. *I know what Mama would do*, she thought. *I know what she did. She ran away. She ran away from it all, except for me. She couldn't take the possibility of being rejected, so she rejected everyone. She thought she knew what people were thinking. And so what kind of life did she have?*

Oh, Mama, Mackie thought, tears trickling down her face. *You were so sad all the time. You were always alone. It was so hard for you to believe that anyone could like you or care about you. And about me, by extension. You could only be safe if we stayed in our small lives with our tiny connections to each other. And that's how you died, Mama.*

Overcome, Mackie collapsed onto the pillows on her porch swing, crying hard. It was all so sad. Poor Mama, dead at forty-nine and never having had a life.

After a while, Mackie lifted her head, aware that Murphy was snuffling on the other side of the front door. She wiped her eyes and drew a big breath. Those grief storms came a lot less often months after Sarah's death, but this one felt different. This felt more like grieving for what Sarah never had. She opened the door for Murph, who bounded out onto the porch and licked her face.

Okay. Crying done. Now she could get down to making a plan.

Mama, she thought, *you didn't dare to live your life. You didn't dare to let anyone know about me. But I'm not you and I have already done what you couldn't do. I can't say it's worked out very well, but I still have done the thing I was so afraid to do. I connected with Eric.*

And so what? her inner critic asked. *What did that get you? Besides yelled at?*

Mackie shook her head. No, she wasn't going back down to that awful space of guilt and self-loathing. She already spent enough time there. She hated herself for not being present when Sarah died, for being unable to stay pregnant, for not being stronger in her marriage, for letting other people run her life. Really, mostly it was her mother and her husband. Letting other people run your life meant that when she needed to act, when she needed to step up and be present for her own mother's death, she had been weak and afraid and she ran away.

Mackie wrote in bright blue pen on her sketch pad: I do not run away.

In red: I no longer run away.

In green: I stay and see things through.

In purple: I stick it out.

In black: I keep my commitments.

Her internal voice mocked her. *No, you don't. Really, who are you kidding?*

Mackie tore off the page and ripped it up. The voice was right. Who was the girl who left her mother to die alone? Who couldn't ask for help while having a miscarriage? Who left her husband rather than try to figure things out? Who came to this charming little town and upended the Johnsons and maybe even kind Declan Kelly, too? Kathy might be nice for now but it was only a matter of time before Eric poisoned her against Mackie. *That's it. It's time to go.*

Mackie headed up the stairs and pulled out her suitcase. She had arrived a few weeks ago with very little, so it took little time to pack.

But the Hamiltons. What about the house?

Her mocking inner voice spoke up again. *I keep my commitments. Yeah, right.*

"Oh, shut up!" Mackie shouted. She knew it was a little crazy to be shouting at her own inner voice, but sometimes it worked. That miserable voice wouldn't let her win, no matter what she did.

Her phone rang. Thank goodness for a distraction. Her own head was making her feel crazy.

"Hi, Declan," she greeted him. "Have I messed up your life?"

He laughed. "I don't think so. Why do you ask?"

"I can't help but think I really messed things up here and I'm trying to decide what to do next. It's a lot to process; I just don't know where I belong."

Declan was silent for a moment. "Maybe you belong where you want to belong," he offered.

She shrugged, then realized once again that he couldn't see her. "Yeah, maybe. So what's up?"

"I wondered if you wanted someone to go to the firefighters' beach party with."

"Beach party?"

"You probably saw the posters. The entire town comes out to celebrate. It's like a local holiday when we hang out on the beach and make an enormous bonfire. People collect money to support the fire department. It'll be fun."

Mackie demurred. "I don't know. I've actually been packing to leave. I honestly think I've done so much damage here that I should just go."

Declan sighed audibly. "Mackie, I think you're wrong about that. I've already given you my opinion on whether you should stay here. I also know that you have to decide for yourself. But at least come to the beach party tonight. You won't be leaving before tomorrow, will you?"

He was right, of course. And she couldn't actually just leave. The Hamiltons were counting on her. The idea of leaving was attractive, but maybe only because that was what she always did. He didn't need to hear all of that though.

"You're right, I won't be leaving tonight. Sure, the beach party sounds okay. I can probably avoid Eric, right? I don't need to get yelled at again."

She could hear relief in Declan's voice, though he tried to keep it light. "So, okay, I'll come and get you. Is eight okay? Full dark is after ten, so the fire part will be late."

"Sure," Mackie said, resigned. She might not leave immediately, but she would start the process. Maybe Cassandra wanted a house-sitting job.

DECLAN ARRIVED ON TIME with a soft-sided cooler and in sneakers. Mackie tossed a windbreaker, water bottle, and a box of her caramel squares into her day pack. They walked the mile to the beach side of the peninsula and started down the hill.

Declan took Mackie's hand. She wanted to pull away—why was he holding her hand?—but she didn't. After a moment it felt completely natural to be walking down the hill toward the beach holding on to Declan's hand, feeling the warmth, the length of his fingers, and his summer calluses from working on the boats. She stole a look at him, wondering what he was thinking. Suddenly a thought rocked her. *This is it. Our last outing together. I'm going back to Massachusetts and Stella Mare is going to keep trying to find a girlfriend for Declan.* Unconsciously, she tightened her grip on his fingers. He looked down at her and smiled.

"Mackie—" he began.

She cut him off. "Declan, let's just go to the beach party. Let me have my last adventure in Stella Mare. I don't know what tomorrow is going to bring and neither do you. Please. Let's just make it fun."

"Of course, Mack," he said. "That's what we're going to do."

The beach was sparsely populated. Even if every single resident was out for the evening, the long beach would never be crowded. But there were blankets, hampers, lots of people near the bonfire pile, and folks making music and singing. Nearby, children played chase with the small waves. The sun was dropping, but there was no pink yet in the sky. The bonfire pile was huge, piled up driftwood and old logs brought down from the woods.

Declan laid out a blanket and dropped his cooler while Mackie slid her day pack off her shoulders. She took out her bottle of water and they turned to the crowd, looking for familiar faces.

Mackie waved to Cassandra and Pat. There were others, too, that she knew. Some she knew by name, while others were familiar faces she had seen in Stella Mare. Thinking about leaving gave her a feeling of nostalgia.

"Hey, girlfriend." Cassandra bounced by. "Saw you show up with Declan, huh? Looking good." Mackie shook her head at her incorrigible friend and turned to Pat.

"Nobody gets to have any privacy around here, do they?" she complained. Pat smiled. "You told me once that secrets are hard to keep in a small town."

"Showing up at a party with a man is like taking out a front-page ad. Especially if that man is the highly attractive and sought-after English teacher," Pat noted. "You can't expect privacy around that. How are you doing otherwise, Mackie? I haven't seen you for a bit."

"Good enough, Pat. Thank you. Thank you so much for talking with me that day. I still don't feel like I know what I'm doing, but at least I am doing something."

Pat nodded and smiled.

That was what Mackie liked about Pat. She didn't want to know all the details. She was just a kind, un-nosy person. Unlike her daughter, who was a kind but very nosy person.

"So, how are things with your *sister*?" Cassandra said to her, sotto voce. Mackie looked at her.

"You were there for our last conversation, Cassandra. Nothing new since yesterday."

"Okay, okay!" Cassandra put up her hand. "You can't blame me for asking."

"Well, maybe I can, but I won't," Mackie said with a smile. "What happens at this event?"

Cassandra excitedly swept her along to meet more friends on the other side of the bonfire pile. Mackie looked back and waved to Declan, who was heading toward friends of his own. Mackie flowed along with the crowd into talk, drinks, and ultimately, toward the music-making on the far side of the beach.

From a distance, she heard guitars and maybe a mandolin, and voices singing. *No fiddling though*, she thought. *Maybe it is safe to go over there.*

The evening flew by as the sun dropped lower and lower. The clouds developed through the range of pinks, roses, and deep purple, until the first twinkles of stars appeared. Mackie stood watching at the edge of the water.

"It's only because it's a peninsula we get sunset over the water," said Declan as he materialized beside her.

Mackie nodded. "Like on Cape Cod. I loved watching the sunset from the Eastham Dunes. This is a treat."

He slid an arm around her shoulder. She felt a little thrill at his casual possessiveness and let the warmth from his skin settle into her. "How's your evening going?" he asked kindly.

"Better than I expected." Mackie nodded. "I have met a lot of good people here. I wish…" She trailed off.

He turned to her, sliding his arm across to rest his hand on her shoulder. "What do you wish, Mackie?" His eyes were warm and loving. She had to look away.

Shaking her head, she said, "Honestly, I don't even know. I don't wish that I had never come, not that. I wish it was still last week, where I was skunking Eric at crib and you and I were biking and hiking and that all the nastiness didn't happen. Silly, I know."

"At the risk of being obvious, we can't go back. I guess the next step involves going somewhere else. Forward?"

"But what direction is forward? That's what I can't figure out. I can't stay here. People are nice enough, but soon everyone will know that Eric can't stand the sight of me and then they'll wish I was gone, too."

"Is that what you heard from Kathy? Eric can't stand the sight of you and that she wishes you were gone? I know better than that, Mack."

"Stop it, Declan. We agreed to go to the party and not have this conversation. I'm sorry I let it get started. Really." She stepped out from under his hand and headed toward the pile of wood. "Come on. Let's go to the bonfire."

"Okay, okay. I'm going to give you space around this, Mackie, but I have an investment in what you decide." She shook her head at him and took off at a trot. He followed.

The mayor made a couple of remarks and the chair of the event thanked the wood carriers, the musicians, and everyone who contributed to the fund for the volunteer fire department. Then the honored guest ceremoniously lit the base of the bonfire pile with a torch. The crowd clapped as the fire sputtered and caught. As the flames leaped upward in the pile so did the cheering.

"And there it is, for another year," said a voice near Mackie. "Now the grown-up party starts." In the dark, it was harder to see who was speaking.

"Oh, hi, Russ," Mackie said.

"Hey, there, Mackie from Massachusetts. Did you bring this big lug with you tonight?" Russ gestured to Declan.

"No, it was the other way around," Mackie explained. "Declan said I shouldn't miss it."

"And you shouldn't, especially as it seems you're practically a local girl," Russ agreed. Local girl? What was he talking about? Mackie felt her shoulders go up and she slipped around to the other side of Declan.

She didn't want to discuss her status with Russ, of all people, the keeper of Eric.

"Hey, Declan," said Russ, "tell her not to worry. Eric's over his mad. She took him by surprise is all."

Declan turned to Russ. "Thanks, Russ. But I don't think this is our topic to discuss."

"Thank you," Mackie breathed to Declan, from his other side.

"Oh, no?" Russ was taken aback. "Okay, then. See you all later."

Mackie was thinking hard. Over his mad? What did that mean? Did he want to see her? Did she want to see him? After all, he threw her out. It probably wasn't up to her to initiate contact. But he was a sick old man. She shook her head again to clear it.

Tonight was a party. That's all. Tonight she was going to just be here in Stella Mare for the traditional beach party and that was all.

The smell of wood smoke mingled with the sea air. Mackie breathed it all in. No matter what happened next, this night was hers. Hers to remember, hers to enjoy. She watched the fire as the largest log burned through and crumbled, making space for more branches to catch. She watched the young teenage boys completely enraptured with the fire poke at it with sticks and get reprimanded by the watchful adults. She felt the sea at her back, the fire in front of her, and her awareness of Declan by her side. *No matter what happens*, she thought, *I am taking tonight to be mine.*

She and Declan made their way back to their blanket and pulled it closer to the fire. Settling down, he pulled a bottle out of the cooler. "Have a drink?" he asked her, taking off the top and handing it to her.

She smiled slowly at him. "A toast?" She offered her bottle. He tapped it with his.

"And what do you propose to toast?" He smiled.

"To this night," Mackie said, "with the sunset, the firelight, the moonrise, the sea air, and just being here. To us just being here. I have nothing more than that."

"Just being us and just being here. I can do that. And that is enough for tonight."

From a distance beyond the fire, a new sound arose. Mackie sat still to listen. "Do you hear something?"

Declan nodded. "Oh, aye. That's fiddling. Eric's probably here."

Mackie took a deep breath. Yes, it was fiddling she could hear. Like a faraway memory, the sound of fiddle music.

"I'm going to stay right here," she said to Declan. "You can go if you want to."

"And why would I do that, Mackie from Massachusetts? You're right here and then so am I." They settled comfortably on the blanket, sipping their drinks, watching the fire and hearing the faraway music. Mackie could feel all the unanswered questions in her belly, but she could also feel something else. Happiness. At this moment, right now, she felt happy.

THE MOON HAD TRAVELED most of its arc before Declan and Mackie gathered their things to walk back up the hill to her place. She let Murphy out for a last run and turned to Declan.

"I hope you'll come in," she said truthfully. "I kind of can't believe I'm saying that, but it's true. Please come in. Stay for a while."

"Sure, I'll come in, Mackie. I'd really like that."

She put on water for tea while Declan let Murph back into the house. The big dog went directly back to bed.

They took their tea into the living room and settled on either end of the comfy couch. Mackie sat facing Declan, legs pulled up under her.

"Thanks for taking me to the party," she started. "I had a great time. I am busy filing it away as a wonderful memory of my time here."

Declan looked into his mug. "You know, you scare me when you talk like that. When you talk like you're already gone. I really want you to stay, Mackie. At least stay for the duration of your house-sitting gig. That was your plan, wasn't it?"

"I really like you, Declan. That was not part of my plan. I'm pretty sure if you knew a little more about me, you wouldn't be so interested in whether I stay or go."

He shook his head. "Mackie, that's not for you to decide. You can decide what you tell me, but you don't get to decide in advance whether I will still like you."

Mackie sighed audibly. Frig. He was right, of course. Here she was doing the same thing with him she had done with Eric and Kathy.

"You're right. Yes, you are right. But this is an old, old pattern for me and I learned it early. Assume that everyone is going to hate you and act accordingly. My mother was brilliant at this, which is why I'm here trying to find anyone in the world that I can belong to." She shook her head, trying to avoid tears. "And I hate feeling sorry for myself. I sound so pitiful. I hate it."

Declan put his cup on the coffee table, then he reached over, took her cup, and set it down, too. He carefully slid his arms around her, all tucked up on the couch, and pulled her toward him. She resisted at first, but then allowed herself to sink into his warmth and let her tears fall. He rocked her gently back and forth until she stopped sobbing and fell into an occasional hiccup.

"Better?" he asked the top of her head. She nodded under his chin.

"But I kind of don't want to move," she said.

"And I don't want you to," he concurred. "But how about a tissue?" She nodded. He fished around and handed her some.

When she'd mopped up her face, she pulled back into her corner of the couch. "Thanks. For tissues, and for being here, and all that."

"Oh, Mackie, it's my pleasure. You just don't know."

She shook her head and looked away. That was hard to take in, that this nice man could find pleasure in holding her and handing her tissues while she cried.

"So," said Declan, with the force of a pronouncement. "What happens now?"

She looked back at his kind face. "Now, I guess I tell you the stuff that I think you won't like. And if you have any of that stuff, maybe you also tell."

"Sounds fair enough to me," Declan agreed. "I'm not much of a mystery, but I keep some things to myself. I know there's talk about why I don't date much. I got a kind of broken heart from someone I went with right after university. But then my uncle needed me to help with fishing and there was a job that suited me at the regional high school, and so I came home. If I have a secret, it's that I write. Probably like most English majors, I have a secret writing life, and honestly, nobody knows. It's not the kind of thing that interests too many folks here, but it consumes a lot of time and energy. So when I'm absent, it's often because I have a deadline."

Mackie smiled. "No secret girlfriends? Cassandra and Kathy want you married off and they probably aren't the only ones."

"The people I spend the most time with are the characters in my books," Declan admitted. "It is a little weird though. Writers don't really make good partners."

"Good to know," Mackie said. "But it's hardly a character flaw. Like being too hardworking is a character flaw."

"What's yours?"

She grimaced. "I thought we established that. I'm always assuming that I know what other people are thinking about me. And that what they think is bad. But, actually, there is another one. Worse, maybe."

He looked at her quizzically. "You'll have to convince me."

"Yeah. Well, I can't be trusted. I leave. Bug out. Disappear when things get tricky. Like I almost did yesterday. When my mother was dying"—her voice caught—"I couldn't even stay in the room with her." Once again, she recalled the surreal feeling of watching the rowers on the Charles River, barely breathing, and getting the phone call with the news. "I left her alone and she died alone. All alone. Because of me."

Her voice caught again. "That—that's probably the worst thing I have ever done. Worse even than telling Eric he had another kid. Worse than leaving my marriage because I didn't want to do what Andrew wanted me to do. I am a leaver, Declan. You cannot count on me to stick around and see it through."

Mackie looked at his face. "I'm going to tell you the whole thing, Declan. Then you'll know all of it." She sounded firmer than she felt.

"So, you know I was married, right? What you don't know is that I almost had a baby. Almost. And then within six months of losing my baby, I lost my mother. And then I found this envelope of letters. I showed you the picture, but the letters are something else. My mother always told me that my father didn't want us, didn't pay child support because he rejected us. This was my mother's world. But when I was clearing out her house, I found these letters to Eric Johnson in Stella Mare and she'd never sent them. Never sent them at all. They were still sealed and stamped. He had no idea. Until I showed up and threw a big thirty-year-old wrench into his life."

Declan sat quietly. Then he reached out to take her hand. "Mackie, what made you come try to find Eric? What happened that made you actually move here, come in person, to find him? That doesn't sound like someone who is always backing away."

"Desperation," she said. "I was desperate. You grew up here. Even after losing your parents, you still had people. A place. You still knew who you were and who your people were. Try to imagine having none of that. My family home was a tiny apartment in a suburb of Boston, where my mother tried her best to raise me. She taught me to be entirely independent or entirely submissive. Do what you are told to do because that is the only way to keep people connected to you. I never had a thought of my own until, well, until things got difficult with Andrew. But when everyone was gone I was truly alone. Mama was dead, really gone, and there was no Andrew and no baby. I knew that I was alone for real."

"Murphy?" asked Declan. "I know he's not a person, but still."

Mackie's face softened. "Oh, Murph. He is a person and he's kept me going. I adopted him against Andrew's better judgment. Getting Murphy was my first big act of resistance. The first thing I did for me. It made the next steps possible. When I found the letters and Stella Mare on the Internet and it was a real place, and Eric was plausibly still around, I decide to embark on an old-fashioned quest. Not an Internet quest, but a real one. And here I am. Not exactly a success."

"Has anyone ever told you that you might be a little hard on yourself?" Declan asked, still holding her hand. "That was a gigantic leap into the unknown. And you stuck it out."

"Yeah. Kathy said that, too." Mackie had to smile. "The day after the kitchen party was hard. You were a big help then. You know, when you're a kid who doesn't know her dad, you spend a lot of time imagining what he might be like. In my eleven- or fourteen-year-old imagination, he was handsome and charming and showered me with presents. He came to rescue me from Mama being overtired and depressed, and from school where I was quiet and had hardly any friends. He was the equivalent of my knight in shining armor. Even though the story my mother told was so terrible, I had this one in my mind."

"Surely you didn't think he would be like you imagined," Declan said. "You're not a kid."

"Surely. I'm not eleven and not fourteen and not even twenty-one. But when I saw him the first time, I realized that all of those fantasies were still with me, still operating. Part of me wanted him to jump up and claim me as his long-lost daughter. I wanted him to take me on as a project. And I think I wanted him to be, well, a lot different from who he really is. Like a lot younger. My mother was only forty-nine when she died last year. It's hard to grasp that he was almost that old when they met."

"You seemed to get along though," Declan noted. "Cribbage and all that."

Mackie laughed a little. "Yeah, that's when I thought that maybe this Eric—even though he would never be my imagined knight—the real Eric who read books and played cribbage and made jokes and played the fiddle, maybe he could still be a father. So I decided to see. And you know what happened there."

"Russ says he's over being mad. And Kathy is pretty happy that you showed up, at least if what I have heard is right. Right?"

"Yeah. But that still doesn't tell me anything about what I should do. I don't feel like I belong here, Declan. Isn't that where this conversation started?"

He pulled her closer. "A long time ago. If I pull this blanket over you, would you go to sleep?"

She smiled and nodded. "And you? Will you stay? I really don't want to be alone right now."

"Of course I'll stay. The couch is big enough for a family of five. I probably won't even crowd your space."

She looked at him warmly. "I don't mind if it's you that's doing the crowding." She turned off the table lamp. They settled into the moonlit dark.

Emergency

Mackie woke up on her corner of the couch. She was suddenly completely awake, even though she'd only been asleep for a few hours. She slid off the blanket and stood, taking a moment to look at Declan asleep at the other end. Her face softened as she took in the waves in his dark hair, the stubble on his face, the shape of his ears. Enough! She tiptoed into the kitchen, closing the door gently behind her.

She filled the electric kettle and turned it on. It was a noisy thing; she'd never noticed before that heating water made so such a racket. Murphy got up off his mat and did his morning stretches, then headed for the back door. She let him out, one ear cocked toward the kettle, noticing the smell of smoke in the dark of the early morning. Leftover bonfire, she thought, and went back in to make tea.

Suddenly the air was rent with sound. There was a huge siren sound outside and Declan's phone started beeping all at once.

Declan banged through the door into the kitchen, phone in hand. "Fire," he stated. "I've got to go. Looks like down on the fishing dock." He reached for Mackie and she hugged him hard.

"Go ahead. I'll be right behind you."

Declan leaped into his truck and backed out of her driveway. *It isn't even properly morning*, Mackie thought, watching him go. The sky was not even starting to become pink. She filled a thermos of full of tea and called the dog into the house.

Mounting her bike, Mackie headed for the shore. Pedaling down the hill, she repeated a mantra. *Let them be safe, let them be safe.* When she got to Main Street, she could already see smoke and flashing lights from the far side of the harbor where the fishing docks were. The fishing docks and the fish houses. Eric's fish house.

Pedaling as close as she could get, she dropped her bike on the grass and trotted toward the crowd of onlookers. There were firetrucks from two villages, police and RCMP cruisers, and visible flames. Mackie saw the volunteer firefighters tackling the blaze. They were in full gear, unrecognizable, but she knew Declan was one of them.

Cassandra and Pat were part of the onlookers; Titus was working to help the men, though from a safe distance, bringing in equipment. Most of the fishers whom she knew from the diner were pitching in. As she watched, the big fish market caught ablaze from the far side.

"Where's the main fire?" she suddenly asked Cassandra. "What's burning?"

Cassandra shrugged. "Looks like everything on the far side of the market, maybe."

A man in front of them turned around and said, "It's not clear. It started somewhere on the other side of the fish market. Don't know if it was the fish and chips stall or what."

Mackie felt a terrible crushing sensation in her chest. The other side of the market was where Eric's family fish house was, where the guys hung out, and where she played cribbage with him. What was happening over there? She couldn't get closer from here, but maybe she would see something if she was on the other side of the harbor. She backed away from the crowd. She needed to head back toward town, or up a hill, or something so that she could see past the market. She started off at a run back toward the village so she could see the arm of the harbor. Breathing hard, she kept looking over her shoulder to see how much was visible. Finally, she had achieved enough elevation to see. And there it was. No flame was yet visible at the market building, but Eric's old wooden fish house was entirely ablaze.

She stood, watching, along with a handful of others, as the fire consumed the structure. When it collapsed, Mackie felt sick. She thought about her recent hours at the fish house, the history of Eric's family, and her own connections there. Gone.

Her crumpling sadness at the loss of the family fish house vied with a sense of relief that at least the building had been empty. The blaze was causing a lot of property damage, but it would be contained to the lower docks and nobody would have been hurt. Mackie headed back toward the scene, sick at heart with her knowledge that the Johnson fish house had not survived the blaze.

But oh, what a mystery! How on earth did this fire begin? She started back toward the crowd, heavy with the feeling of loss. More loss, of course, for the townspeople. She wondered what it was like for them to watch fire consume the harbor buildings.

As Mackie approached the scene, shouting arose from the crowd, nearly as loud as the sirens and roaring fire. Something else was happening. The shouting got louder and louder and not only because she was getting closer.

As she got closer to the onlookers, words became clearer. "There's somebody in there!"

"Oh my goodness! Who is it? Who would be out here this time of night?"

"What can they do? Nobody could go into that inferno now. Who knows how bad it is inside?"

"Can they rescue them? What's happening?"

Oh, no. Her relief about nobody being hurt had been premature. Get whom out of where? She thought of all the fishers at the diner in the early morning, who'd welcomed her with questions and comments, who pushed Declan her way, who wandered in and out of her consciousness while she was paying attention to Eric. Who could it be?

"What's going on?" she asked breathlessly. Nobody answered, so she shook the sleeve of the man nearest to her. "What's happening?" she demanded.

He looked down at her absently. "Somebody in the market building, they think. No reason for it. But still they think there's somebody in there. Makes more sense for someone to be in a fish house or boat house at this hour. Nobody could survive the fire at the Johnson fish house though. At least the market building isn't fully engaged."

There was a general surge of the crowd as another wailing ambulance arrived, making the onlookers split and separate. Across the way, the emergency workers were busy, clearing space, keeping the crowd back, hauling hoses, working quickly and efficiently. Mackie pushed her way through the crowd, looking for someone, anyone, who could tell her anything more. She found Pat and Cassandra again. They had no further information to share.

"I feel so helpless. Everyone is working so hard. Isn't there anything we can do?" demanded Mackie.

Pat shook her head. "Pray, maybe, if you're so inclined."

Cassandra suddenly said, "Yes, I know what we can do. Let's find Sonny. Coffee. Everyone is going to need coffee. We can get coffee on the scene."

Pat nodded. "Good idea. That's a practical way to help. You two can get that started."

Mackie and Cassandra pushed through the crowd looking for Sonny. The owner and chef at Sunshine's was already heading back toward the village to the diner.

"Sure, come on girls," he said. "We can help the best way we know how." The three started toward Main Street. Before they were out of earshot, though, Mackie heard a shout, picked up and carried by the watching crowd. "It's old Eric! Eric is in the fire. They've got to get old Eric out!"

In shock, Mackie stared at Cassandra. The younger woman gave her a push back toward the crowd. "Get back there, girl. Sonny and I got the coffee. Go on. You go and see." Mackie ran back toward the crowd.

It was hard to see anything in the crush of people, the smoke and the dim predawn light. She pushed her way through the crowd, mumbling apologies and making her way up to the police tape that kept spectators at a safe distance.

As she came closer, she saw a firefighter coming out of the big fish market building. He was struggling to carry someone draped across his arms. The firefighter stumbled, then righted himself and barreled down the ramp. As soon as he was clear of the building, two other firefighters arrived to help, and the paramedics took charge of the limp figure. As they lifted the burden, the rescuer's knees seemed to buckle. His fellow firefighters each took an elbow to support him as he stumbled toward the other ambulance. They helped him sit on a bench next to the vehicle. One of the paramedics brought oxygen to him. As he pulled off his helmet, the watching crowd recognized him.

"Declan. It was Declan brought him out," said a voice in the crowd. "You know, the teacher." More people took up his name. Declan brought the victim out. Declan rescued the person left in the market. Declan! Declan was being treated by the paramedics and so was the victim. Mackie stared, trying to make sense of what she was seeing.

She had no way to confirm who Declan had rescued. Was that Eric? The paramedics strapped the person onto a gurney, oxygen mask over the face. They slid the patient into the ambulance, leaped aboard, and with a blip of the siren, glided through the crowd. Mackie looked with shock at the departing ambulance.

"Who was that?" she asked, wildly. "Did you see? Do you know who that was?"

The man beside her looked toward her kindly. "Somebody said it was Eric Johnson. Can't really tell though. Looks like Declan Kelly pulled him out. Oh, watch out! Looks like the building is going to go."

A TALISMAN OF HOME

Police officers pushed the townspeople back toward the street, keeping them safely away from the scene. An enormous roar startled Mackie as part of the roof of the market fell in.

The water finally started to make headway on the flames, and the fury of the fire abated. Firefighters continued to spray the building and the police encouraged onlookers to go home, get some sleep. Somebody mentioned that the Sunshine had free coffee and there was a noticeable thinning of the crowd. Daylight was coming.

Things were calming down at the scene, but Mackie's insides were still wound up. The first ambulance was gone, the siren still loud in Mackie's memory. If Eric was in that ambulance, Kathy needed to know. Mackie fumbled for her phone.

Looking up, she saw Declan standing and sipping water outside the barricade, leaning against a truck in the parking lot. He looked up at her and waved. She walked toward him. He was smoke-smeared and exhausted. He was also jubilant.

"Mackie!" He struggled to stand upright in his gear. She gazed at him like he was brand new. "He was breathing, Mack, when I got him. He was still alive. It was Eric and he was still breathing."

"You—you were amazing," she says, staring at his dark brown eyes. It was as if she had not really seen him before.

Declan blurted, "You have to go to the hospital, Mack."

Jolted out of her reverie, she agreed. "So it really was Eric. Yes, I have to go, and Kathy..."

"I called Kathy," Pat said from behind her. "What can I do to help?"

Mackie looked around. "Uh, I brought my bike. Can you take me to the hospital?"

"No, that's okay, Pat," Declan said. "I have to stay here and help secure the site. Mackie, why don't you take my truck and I'll meet you there later?" He tossed her the keys and she nodded, again, wordless.

Pat took the keys and Mackie's arm. "Come on, Mackie, I'll show you where to go."

FOLLOWING PAT'S DIRECTIONS, Mackie drove the half hour, following signs for the hospital. The parking lot for the emergency room was full, even now, shortly after dawn. Mackie remembered to lock Declan's truck and ran to the entry. The waiting area was full and there was a bustle of activity. Maybe there were other people hurt by the fire, Mackie thought absently, but her only concern was Eric.

At the triage desk, Mackie waited for a nurse to finish taking someone's information. Impatient, Mackie grabbed the sleeve of a passing man in scrubs. "Where's the guy they brought in from Stella Mare? From the fire?" she demanded with a shaky voice. He shook his head and continued on his way.

She had to sit and wait for her turn to talk to the nurse. Her impatience was overwhelming and her mind raced with all the possible outcomes. She could barely contain herself. The half hour wait felt forever.

When she finally got to the triage nurse, she asked for Eric by name. "Eric Johnson. The man who came in from the fire. Can I see him?"

The nurse looked at her. "This is emergency treatment. Nobody's getting visitors here. If you want to visit a patient, you need to come back later today."

"No, no. I just need to know if he's okay?" Mackie didn't remember ever feeling so panicked. The nurse, Paul, seemed unperturbed by her distress.

"We don't give out information about our patients. Are you a family member?" Paul asked, turning toward his laptop. Mackie felt shock. How to answer that question?

"Uh, well," she started, then immediately began to cry. "Yeah, I think so."

Taking pity, Paul said, "Listen, I can't tell you anything about anyone here. But I can tell you that the family waiting room for surgery is down the hall to the left." He pointed out the way.

"Thank you, thank you!" Surgery! At least that meant he was alive! Mackie almost danced down the hall. What an emotional rollercoaster.

Mackie peered around the corner into the family waiting room. Kathy was there with Jake. *They both look disheveled*, Mackie thought, *but no more than me*. She wondered how long they had been waiting. They looked up when she stepped into the room.

Jake handed Kathy a cup of coffee and turned back to the machine to get another. Kathy stared at Mackie.

"Mackie. You don't have to be here."

Moving toward her, Mackie asked, "How is he? What do they know?"

Jake answered. "Not much. Something maybe fell on him; he's busted up some and had lots of smoke inhalation. We don't really know much." Kathy looked into her coffee cup and sighed.

"Mackie," she started. "I know you want to be able to talk to Dad. But now's not the time."

Before Mackie could respond, there was a stir at the doorway. Someone in scrubs asked for Kathy. Kathy gave Jake a look, took a big breath, and headed toward the door.

After Kathy left, more people arrived. Declan, along with Terence and Tate, Kathy and Jake's twin teens, entered the room. Mackie noticed the boys were tall, even taller than Jake, and lanky.

"How's Grandpa?" asked Tate, moving toward his father. "Mum was talking to someone out there."

Jake hugged his son and said, "Grandpa's in surgery, kids."

Declan headed straight for Mackie and wrapped his arms around her. She felt his strength, noticed the warmth of his arms, the clean fresh smell from his recent shower. She allowed herself to be held; at least someone was glad she was here.

They got coffee and sat on the uncomfortable vinyl chairs.

Kathy came back in, looking exhausted. Terence went to her with a hug. Mackie could see Kathy holding back tears.

"We still don't know anything. No, there is no bad news. They just needed my signature on some stuff," she responded to the questions. "We're still waiting. They're still checking things out."

"But he's alive?" Mackie asked in a whisper.

Kathy gave her a hard look. "Yup. Somehow.

"Declan," Kathy said, voice shaking. "Declan, what you did..." Declan stood while Kathy hugged him hard. "They said it was you who brought him out." She pulled back a little to look him full in the face. "I can't even tell you what that means."

Declan's eyes were glittering, too. "Aw, Kath, that's what we do, right? I'm just glad he's still with us." Jake came over and joined them.

"Yeah, Declan, that was going beyond. Maybe a little foolish," Jake said, clapping Declan on the back before returning to his position leaning on the counter next to the coffee machine. "But the best kind of foolish. I'm glad you're okay, boy."

In the next hour, Russ arrived with Jimmy. "How's our old guy?" he asked.

Kathy shrugged. "We're waiting. Still waiting." The men settled in to wait, too.

Declan and the twins huddled over one of their cell phones talking about high school. Kathy fretted in her chair. Jake paced.

As time dragged on, Mackie became more and more uncomfortable. Kathy wasn't talking to her and Declan was absorbed in his young cousins. What right, really, did she have to be here? She wasn't part of the family. She was just the new girl who said she was Eric's daughter. Kathy thought she was trying to get a chance to talk to Eric. She had no idea what other people might think. She wondered why she was sitting in this room like she belonged here. The last she knew Eric was furious at her and denying everything.

Okay, there were hints of other things, like Kathy had been kind of welcoming and Russ said Eric was over being mad. But Mackie's last image of Eric was his angry face as he tipped the card table in the fish house.

Oh, the fish house. The fire. The overwhelming events of the last hours felt crushing.

She desperately wanted to leave. Her mind made images of places she'd rather be: hiking with Murphy, sitting on her couch with a cup of tea, back in Somerville walking to the library, even along the bank of the Charles waiting for Sarah to die.

No, not that, she thought. *No, no, no. I am no longer that person. See it through.*

This is different from Mama though. Mama was all alone. I really abandoned her. Eric has his family here, more or less. And he threw me out. He'd probably throw me out again if he had the opportunity. Leaving now wouldn't be abandoning Eric. He doesn't want me here anyway.

She stood up and walked slowly toward the hallway. She stopped at the doorway and turned to look back into the family waiting room. She felt the tug of the freedom to leave, the sense of relief she would feel in driving away. She saw Kathy, leaning back in her chair, tear stains on her cheeks. She watched Jake peering into his empty coffee cup. And Declan, taking a moment from his conversation with Terence to look up at her and smile. She felt a connection to them all. It really didn't matter whether Eric wanted her there or not, Mackie realized. He wasn't there to share his opinion. With a sudden clarity, Mackie felt it. She wanted to be there with Kathy and Jake, with the kids, and with Declan. She wanted to be there for Mackenzie Brown who did have a father. Mackenzie Brown who did not run away.

Mackie could still feel the urge to run away. But she was staying. She moved back into the waiting room and sat down near Declan. She would continue to stay. Kathy and Declan both knew, for sure, that Mackie was Eric's daughter. Declan knew also that Mackie had fallen short before when her mother was dying. He knew that she was testing her determination. His knowledge of her past and her plan for the present, and the warm smile he sent her way helped Mackie feel more confident about her decision. *I'm here*, she thought firmly. *I'm staying*.

They had all been waiting for what seemed like forever when the surgeon stopped by to talk with Kathy. They spoke quietly by the door with everyone else watchfully silent. When she turned back to the waiting family, she looked devastated.

"Kath?" Jake reached for her hand. "What's going on?"

"They're putting him in intensive care for now," she said. "He's not doing too well. They fixed up the fractures. They kind of stuck the parts back together, but he is not in good shape. And there's more. Jake, Dad's sick. He's a lot sicker than I knew. The cancer, you know. But they're going to let me see him just for a minute."

Kathy headed down the hall with another nurse. Jake slumped in a chair, hands between his legs. The kids were suddenly somber. Mackie sat, face in her hands, with Declan beside her, just sitting and waiting.

Kathy came back within a few minutes. She looked grim, but slightly less scared. "It's okay, guys," she said to her boys and Jake. "You all can go home. It's well past lunchtime, isn't it? Or maybe just get outside for a walk or something."

She sat down by Declan and Mackie, stretched in the chair, then asked Declan to go get her some more coffee.

"Not from here, Declan," she insisted. "Go down to the cafeteria and get me a latte."

"Kath, send one of the kids," he said. She shook her head.

"No, Declan, you go. I want to talk to Mackie."

He frowned.

"I insist," she said. "I need to talk to her."

Declan left but not without a backward glance at Mackie, who nodded. Then Kathy turned her attention to Mackie.

"I don't think he's going to be awake for a while. I don't know that you'll have a chance to talk to him. You don't really have to be here, you know. It's just family here and I suspect it is really just a waiting game."

"Waiting game? Like you think he's going to die?"

Kathy looked away. "It isn't looking good. He's got a bunch of things wrong with him, like cirrhosis, for one, and then it turns out that his cancer has returned and he didn't tell me. Didn't tell anyone. Dad has always been good at not telling us stuff that he figured was private. As you know."

"And there was stuff he didn't even know. Like me."

They looked at each other. Kathy nodded. "Yes, like you."

Mackie drew a deep breath. "Kathy, my mother is dead. I told you that. And there is more that you don't know. I've lost everyone in my life. So I came here to try to find out if there was anyone left, even someone who I never knew."

"And what did you find?" Kathy leaned back in her chair.

"Well, Eric, obviously, even if he won't claim me. But also, you."

Declan appeared in the doorway holding a cardboard tray of coffee cups. He took one look at both women and stepped back down the hallway.

"I know I probably don't really belong here with the family, especially since he made it clear that I had to go." Mackie's throat tightened as she spoke. She wanted to hide under the chair, leave the building, run as fast as she could on the beach until she collapsed, breathless. The desire to get out of the room was overwhelming. "But you and he are all I have. My mother is dead and there is nobody else. I know you don't want me here."

Her chest was about to burst when Kathy turned toward her. Her voice was gentle. "Well, Mackie, maybe we need you here."

She dared to look at Kathy's face. Kathy's blue eyes were looking at her. It felt like they were looking right into her. They were warm and kind and filling with tears. Mackie felt tears of her own when Kathy's hand found hers.

Kathy spoke softly. "I think this is going to be a hard time with Dad. It would be good to have a sister to help out."

Mackie nodded, furiously dashing tears off her cheeks with the back of her other hand.

"How could it be that Dad didn't know? That seems impossible," Kathy wondered out loud.

Mackie shrugged. "My mother said he was never interested, so she left him alone. I found all these letters she had written to him, but she'd sent none of them. That's how I knew who to look for. So I think he didn't even know until I picked the worst day to try to talk with him."

Kathy frowned. "You didn't know it was the worst day, Mackie. Tell me about what happened."

Mackie stumbled. "Yeah. I went to play cribbage with him on Thursday, but I didn't want to play cribbage. Instead, I showed him this picture." She pulled the snapshot out of her pocket where it was crumpled. She smoothed it out for Kathy to see.

"Is this your mum?" Kathy asked softly. "She was so young. Younger than my Simon."

"Yes. She was only nineteen when I was born. That was the summer after she finished high school. She was working in Bar Harbor."

"And look at Dad," Kathy marveled. "He was a handsome guy, wasn't he? That was one of those summers we didn't see him at all, I think."

"There's more," Mackie said. She pulled the medallion off over her head, handing it to Kathy.

"What is this?"

"Nothing, really," Mackie said. "It's just a souvenir from Bar Harbor the summer they were together. I found it hidden in my mother's things, along with the snapshot and the letters. My mother was pretty ashamed of being pregnant at nineteen and I guess her family was not much good about that either. She left her family and never told Eric and she just went to Boston, pregnant and alone. She just shoved the complete history away and got on with it."

Kathy's face was compassionate. "Except there was a baby to consider."

Mackie felt her eyes filling up again. "Yeah, that."

"What did you say to him?"

"I was hoping to let him draw the conclusion, I guess. I didn't come right out and say, 'Hey, Eric, you're my father.' But I did tell him that I was born in April of 1986 while he was holding the picture and the medallion. It was kind of obvious at that point." Mackie looked at the floor. "He was furious. He threw the picture back at me, flipped the table over, spilling coffee everywhere, and told me to get out. He was frightening, really."

"Oh, honey," Kathy crooned and wrapped Mackie in a big hug. "He's such a bear at times. You surprised him for sure. I have to admit that you surprised me, too. But for me it seems like a good thing. I am happy to have you in the family, Mackie. I thought I was going to have to count on Declan to bring you in, but here you are."

Mackie pulled away with a laugh. "Declan!"

"Yeah, I had you two married off in my imagination. You had no idea, I'm sure. But I'll let you guys handle that, since it looks like you're here to stay, at least in the family."

Mackie felt her heart warming to Kathy's words. She could stay in the family. Kathy wanted her.

Kathy grinned. "It might take a little getting used to having a sister, especially one so much younger than me, but I think I will like it."

Pulling Together

Mackie woke to a beautiful summer day, feeling almost like singing. She threw on her jacket to take Murphy out for his walk as the fog was still hanging around, though sunshine was nearly ready to break through. Before she'd left the hospital last night, the doc said that Eric was improving, though he was still not conscious or breathing on his own. Kathy and Jake had sent Mackie and Declan home. Declan drove Mackie home in his truck and dropped her off where Murphy was delighted to see her after a long, long day of being alone.

As she hiked up the hill into the woods with the dog, she had a lot of things to think about. She had gone from being a woman alone, with no family at all, to being a sister. And having a sister. A sister!

A sister who was ten years older and who had grown-up children. A sister who had her own history with Eric and her own life without him. A sister who didn't automatically hate her for just being born, no matter what Mackie had expected.

And Declan. Declan was so important to her now. No matter what happened to them in the future, Declan had saved her father. He had been the first person to know that Eric was Mackie's father, and he kept her secret well. He was even there to help her when she needed it. And he was most decidedly interested in her, and she herself was not immune to the warm feelings that flowed in her whenever he was around. Mackie had a strong sense that her future life and Declan's would be connected somehow, even if only because his cousin was married to her sister. Her sister, Kathy!

And Eric. What about Eric? It was harder to get her mind around Eric and all that had happened. Eric might still be mad. He might be unwilling to accept her. But more critical than that, he might not survive this medical crisis. Mackie knew acutely that "doing better" was not the same as "doing well."

She felt a stab of pain near her heart as she thought about losing her chance to connect with Eric. To have come so far and to still miss out on the opportunity to be a family would be so painful. Mackie felt her tears start again at the thought. Eric might not pull through. Kathy had said he was seriously ill otherwise, too. Mackie hoped with desperation for him to recover, for his own sake, of course, but also she could have the conversation she longed for.

The inner voice showed up, as usual. *All about you*, it sneered. *You already tried to have that conversation, Mackenzie. Remember what happened? He doesn't want you.*

She shook her head. Today was not the day for internal criticism. Eric might be angry about her, but Kathy wasn't, and Eric might come around in time. Maybe some family was better than no family, and a sister could be better than a father anyway, if you couldn't have both.

Oh, Mama, Mackie thought, feeling her familiar anger, *why did you put me in this position? Why didn't you stay connected to family? Why didn't you let Eric know about me? How hard could that have been?* She reached the top of the trail and stepped out into summer sunshine. Dropping to sit on the rocky outcrop, she pulled out her snapshot again.

There was her mother, impossibly young, and Eric, well over forty, already going gray, but full of life and energy. There they were, a couple that should never have been. Eric was probably as old as Sarah's father, Mackie thought for the first time. What was she seeing, at nineteen, that made her go head over heels? Mackie remembered her mother, small and quiet, working all week, making crafts for sale on the weekends, pinching every penny, and always so watchful over Mackenzie.

No, Kenzie, you can't go to their house. I don't know them. No, Kenzie, it's not polite to ask for something to eat. Kenzie, nice girls look to see how they can be helpful. Kenzie, watch out for people. Everyone doesn't have your back like Mama does. Don't worry, Kenzie, those girls are just mean. Mama can be your friend. You don't need them.

That summer of 1985 must have been a time that felt full of promise, Mackie thought. Sarah was out of her parents' house, on her own for the first time, really. And here was handsome Eric, all attentive to the quiet, shy girl from Dover-Foxcroft.

And what was it like for her, Mackie wondered, to realize in the fall that she was pregnant? Pregnant? Mackie knew that her mother had been enrolled in community college and then abruptly left to move to Boston. Sarah had told her daughter that her own parents were dead and that she had no other family.

Mackie had never questioned that. Sarah was her family and she was Sarah's family. That was all. But being here in Stella Mare made Mackie realize that family can mean a lot of different things. Didn't anyone in the town of Dover-Foxcroft, Maine, notice when nineteen-year-old Sarah disappeared to Boston? Didn't anyone care?

Abruptly, Mackie scrambled to her feet and called to Murphy. She took off down the path toward her house. How had she never asked these questions before? Why did she just take Sarah at face value, even after discovering that she had fabricated Eric's response to the pregnancy?

ARRIVING AT THE HOUSE, she impatiently tapped her foot as her laptop booted up.

Sarah Brown of Dover-Foxcroft, Maine, abruptly disappeared in the fall of 1985. Really? Can that actually happen?

A TALISMAN OF HOME

Mackie opened a search page and typed in "Missing girl Dover-Foxcroft 1985," and hit the enter key. She got up and filled the electric kettle, too impatient to sit and wait for results.

Clicking the kettle on, she peered at the screen. No Sarah Brown, but a thirteen-year-old girl had been lost and then found. She broadened her search to missing persons. This netted a hit on the Maine State Police page, where they were highlighting unsolved missing persons cases as far back as the 1980s.

Mackie scanned the twenty or so photos of people, looking for a familiar face. There were mostly boys and a few older men, but no, look! There she was. Her mother, probably a high school picture, with that tousled hair so ubiquitous in the 1980s. There was her mother, a missing person! She clicked on the picture to find more information. There must have been a family in order for a missing persons case to be opened.

Her click-through on her mother's picture pulled up a file. This missing person, while indubitably her mother, wasn't Sarah Brown. Instead, it was Linda Spaulding. Linda. Eric had been right about the name. It was Linda Spaulding who had that summer with Eric in Bar Harbor. But it was Sarah Brown who was Mackie's mother.

Mackie dug in to do some research on Linda Spaulding, and yes, she found more pictures of a girl who had been her mother. Why had she never thought to do this before? Mackie knew why, but didn't want to acknowledge it. She had been so much a part of her mother's carefully crafted fictional isolation that she never tried to shake it. Even finding the letters to Eric didn't loosen her belief that her mother was fundamentally honest. That her mother was alone and therefore she, Mackenzie, was also alone. Why this elaborate deception? Who was Linda and why did she leave? What made her turn into Sarah?

Now, for the first time, Mackie wondered what Eric could tell her about her mother. For so long, Eric had been the mystery, but now it felt like Sarah had been the one to keep the secrets.

Mackie poked around a little more, this time checking newspaper archives. The *Piscataquis Observer* was the paper of record. In December 1985 there was a brief note that Linda Spaulding was missing, last seen on her way to community college on November 22. She had never been located.

She kept scrolling back through the archives, looking for Spauldings and for Browns, until she hit something. Pay dirt? They had arrested Laurence Spaulding for a domestic disturbance in 1980. Laurence? And there was more. Gary Spaulding (related?) was convicted of child molestation. In 1985. After Linda left home, Mackie realized. What had happened?

Mackie poked back further into birth records. Linda Spaulding, born in 1966, child of Laurence and Hilda, baptized at St. Thomas Aquinas Catholic Church. Oh, maybe this. What would it mean to Laurence and Hilda if their Linda were pregnant? Laurence seemed to have a history of meanness; Mackie could understand the challenge faced by a young woman with strict and angry parents.

But was being pregnant enough of a reason to disappear? It seemed likely. Shame to the family and all of that. Mackie knew better than anyone how hard her mother had worked to avoid shame, at least the shame of rejection.

Now Mackie had a new story to integrate. Linda, age nineteen, had a wonderful summer with an older man in 1985. She found herself pregnant but didn't tell anyone. Instead, she just disappeared, changed her name, and moved to the relative anonymity of the city. She didn't even tell the father of the child, who was nearly as old as Linda's own father. She had assumed he would shame and reject her, just as she expected shaming and rejection from her parents. Maybe it had actually happened that way. Maybe she told her parents and they chased her away. Mackie's eyes stung just thinking about that.

But that was not really Sarah's way. Instead, she was more likely to have done with her parents exactly what she did with Eric. Linda, later known as Sarah, assumed the worst. Then she ran away. She rejected her parents and Eric before they could reject her. She took care of herself. But at a terrible cost, thought Mackie.

Mackie shook her head. *Oh, Mama. What a mess. Maybe I have grandparents in Maine as well as a father and sister right here. Maybe we didn't have to be alone for the last thirty years.*

The sheer tragedy of never knowing struck Mackie like a blow. Sarah had never known if her parents and Eric would accept her pregnancy. Mackie had never known she even had these family members. And they had never known of her existence.

Every family has its secrets, Pat had said. Maybe some secrets should be kept. Maybe some secrets kept people from suffering. Mackie knew that her mother had believed that. Mackie was now seeing it differently though. Some secrets just led to more sadness and tragic loss.

It didn't take long to find death notices for both Laurence and Hilda Spaulding. They died within a year of each other, Mackie noted, in 1999. They never got to know what happened to their daughter, Linda. What was it like to live with that ambiguous loss for fourteen years? What a toll that must have taken and it was so unnecessary.

Mackie couldn't imagine a situation in which Sarah couldn't have taken her home to meet her grandparents. Either they were truly terrible people or Sarah was so fearful of rejection that she couldn't risk it. Even with the newspaper note about Laurence's arrest, Mackie felt certain that her mother's fears were the reason for never going back. She wondered if Sarah knew when her parents died and why she never spoke of that to her daughter. Mackie felt stunned, again, by the weight of Sarah's secrets.

Feeling heavy and sad for her mother and that family in Maine, Mackie no longer had the energy to feel angry. She thought about how Sarah had pushed her into things that were meant to save her, but ultimately created more heartache. She had meant well. She was just afraid.

Of everyone and everything. Most important to her had been protecting her beloved Kenzie.

Sarah hadn't even considered dating or marriage while she was busy raising her daughter. Despite that, Sarah pushed Kenzie into an early marriage, reminding her always to accommodate and be willing to sacrifice for her husband. She wanted Kenzie to have what she didn't have for herself. *The way to keep your man? Take good care of your husband lest he leave you behind. Your primary job is to keep him happy, so you won't be alone.*

As a consequence, Kenzie had done whatever Andrew wanted and it was fine. Except the dog. And the baby. Mackie didn't want to go back to those memories, but they always erupted in her brain on a continuous loop.

Andrew never wanted children. He had said that from the start and when she got pregnant, he insisted on an abortion. For the first time in her life, Mackenzie said no. He said it was necessary to their marriage; she decided that the marriage was not as important as this child.

She remembered the moment when that become clear to her. Andrew was standing at the door of their bedroom, leaning against the door frame. He was impossibly beautiful, as usual. Blond hair and green eyes, body lean and strong, tanned from a summer on the golf course. His eyes were hard though.

"Have you taken care of it yet?"

She was shaking, curled up on the bed with a book, a cozy blanket spread over her.

"What do you mean taken care of it?" She knew exactly what he meant.

"Kenzie, I told you that our marriage is off if you don't end this pregnancy. I don't even know how you got pregnant. Is there something you want to tell me?"

She made a disgusted noise. "I got pregnant the usual way, Andrew. With you. With our baby. Doesn't that mean anything to you?"

He shook his head. "Don't start. We agreed from the beginning. No kids. Nothing to get in the way. I have plans for my life and this is not part of it."

She sat silent, shocked.

Andrew had pulled his phone out of his pocket. "Do you need help to do this? I can make an appointment for you." He turned away and started to talk on the phone. Kenzie got off the bed and slammed the door behind him. She phoned Mama.

"Kenzie, you need to listen to your husband," Sarah entreated her. "He knows what's best for you."

"Mama, can you hear yourself?" Kenzie was incensed again. "What if somebody said that to you when you were expecting me?"

Sarah was quiet. "Mama?" Kenzie checked in. "Mama, are you still there?"

"Yes, I'm here." Sarah's voice was quieter now. "Kenzie, you know I would never want to be without you. But I don't want you to live the kind of life I have, always being on my own. Listen to your husband. He's your husband, you know. For better or worse."

Mackie shook her head, coming out of the reverie. Someone HAD said that to Sarah, now she was sure of it. But Sarah or Linda or whoever had decided that keeping the baby was the right thing for her, even if nobody else agreed. Or, more likely, she didn't give anyone a chance to agree or disagree. She just left.

There was no abortion. There was no further discussion either. Kenzie started separation proceedings and Andrew moved out of their little house. But within four weeks, Kenzie lost her pregnancy and Sarah had a new diagnosis of pancreatic cancer, and only a few weeks to live.

In a matter of months, Kenzie lost her baby, her husband, and her mother. Maybe she lost her husband first, because he was never really there for her.

Then, in the moments when her mother was dying, she literally left the building, ran away, overwhelmed. Within the hour, she was completely alone, more powerfully alone than she ever thought possible.

Not for the first time, Mackie noted that her own tendency to cope by leaving might be a family trait. But not this time. She would not leave this time.

It had been a massive leap of faith to come to Stella Mare. It was a crazy idea that arose when she found the manila envelope with the letters, the picture, and the medallion. Maybe she was not truly alone in the world. Maybe she could still have someone in her life, even though she was painfully aware of her own shortcomings. She remembered Kathy's kind face, and her blue eyes filling with tears as she said, "It would be good to have a sister."

Her inner voice was gearing up to tell her all the things wrong with her. But now was not the time to sink into the familiar pit of self-criticism. She was here in Stella Mare, where her father was struggling for life, where her half sister was happy to know of her existence, and where a lovely man seemed to really like her. She would not let that internal berating start. She was going to be the sister that Kathy thought she was. She was going to be the woman she knew she could be.

Mackie was good at too much thinking, but too much thinking wasn't good for her. This time, she called a halt to thinking. She got up and headed toward the door. She stopped at the sight of Declan walking purposefully toward her porch.

She met him halfway and he wrapped her in his arms instantly.

"I was just thinking about you," she told him, tipping her head back to look at him.

He gently cupped her face in his hand. "And I keep thinking about you. How are you holding up?"

She leaned into him. "Better like this," she admitted. Her phone buzzed in her pocket.

Kathy.

"We're at the hospital, Mackie. I think you should come."

She looked at Declan and they headed off toward the truck. "On our way."

As they drove down the shore road, Mackie was talkative.

"Maybe he's awake," Mackie wondered out loud to Declan. He drove fast. His face looked little tight around the eyes. Mackie put it down to fatigue.

"I wonder if it makes a difference to him that Kathy is okay with me being around?" She continued to think out loud. "Maybe he's less mad at me now. Or maybe I am just optimistic."

"Well, regardless of what he says, you're here and Kathy's good with you," Declan stated. "And Kathy is just the beginning, you know. Her kids are your nephews, and she has cousins probably, too. You might have lots of relatives. Maybe you can decide to stay for a while. Imagine, Stella Mare might be your home. Plus, it would be highly irresponsible to leave your homeowners without a house sitter, you know." He grinned at her sideways.

"Hmm." She smiled. "Is that what you were thinking? It's very kind of you to consider the needs of the Hamilton family, who aren't even here." *Wow*, Mackie thought. *I'm actually flirting.*

"I've been very clear about my ulterior motive, Mackie," he said. "Let me know if I get too obvious."

The two of them continued with the light chatter as they walked into the hospital. Jake was waiting for them in the lobby. "They have moved him to a new unit. You go ahead in, Mackie," he said kindly to her. "They want the family to come in. Remember where we were last night? That room. Declan and I will get some coffee."

She turned to look at Declan. This wasn't what she expected. They wanted the family? This didn't sound optimistic. She hurried down the corridor to the family waiting room.

Kathy and her children were talking with a new doctor. Mackie walked hesitantly in. "Oh, there she is," Kathy exclaimed. "Come on over, Mackie. Dr. Aram is updating us."

Kathy turned back to Dr. Aram. "This is my sister, Mackie," she said. Mackie felt a warm rushing in her chest as she looked at Kathy and her big, strapping teenage sons. "We all need to know what's happening with Dad."

Dr. Aram nodded. "Hello. I was just telling Kathy that your father has been struggling a lot today and, even though he's managed breathing on his own, he is not likely to recover much more. He breathed in a lot of smoke, and of course had the fractures, and a rib punctured one lung. He's been followed by Dr. Carrigan in oncology, who reported last week on probable cancer in several organs. He's at risk for liver failure, too. With your permission, we will move him into a palliative care bed, as he is quite fragile from a medical point of view. He's unlikely to survive any treatment for all the things that are ailing him."

"Yes, of course," Kathy said. "Yes, you have my permission."

Mackie looked at Kathy. Unlikely to survive treatment? Palliative care? This wasn't what she expected to hear. She thought maybe he was awake, talking. Now they were putting him in palliative. She struggled to take it all in. Dr. Aram noted her glance. "I'm going to send Cynthia to talk to you. She's our palliative care social worker. She'll help you make some decisions about this." Dr. Aram walked away. Mackie looked again at Kathy.

"I don't understand. I thought he was better."

Kathy nodded. "Better than he was last night, I think is what they meant. He was okay to leave intensive care. Let's sit down," she suggested. Turning to Terence and Tate, she said, "Why don't you guys go find your dad and Declan and get some doughnuts across the street?"

The boys jumped up with alacrity. Tate looked at his mother. "But Mum, are you alright?"

She nodded. "Yes, go ahead, kids. Mackie's here with me," Kathy said.

The boys headed off. She gave a short laugh. "Food and teenage boys. You can always keep them busy by feeding them. Hospitals and old people and dying... I'm sure that doughnuts sound a lot better than this."

"Dying?" asked Mackie. "Is Eric dying? I'm not ready... I thought you called me to come see him because he was better."

Tears started again in Mackie's eyes. Why was she crying about this man who yelled at her, who refused to acknowledge her, who was just an old guy dying in a bed down the hall? Mackie mopped at her eyes. "I seem to cry all the time." She sniffled. "I'm not always like this, honest."

Kathy looked at her sympathetically. "I don't think we're going to get good news, really, Mackie. I think we can just do our best to make things as easy as possible. I know that's not what you were hoping for."

Mackie shook her head. "Yeah. What I wanted isn't relevant at this point though. Thanks for calling me."

Kathy raised her eyebrows. "Family. You're with us."

"Mrs. Kelly, Ms. Brown? Hi, I'm Cynthia. Dr. Aram asked me to talk to you a little about our palliative care unit and your dad." The woman was about forty, with warm brown eyes and a gentle voice. "He's going into our palliative unit. Do you know about palliative care?" she inquired.

Mackie nodded. "My mother was in palliative in Boston," she told the social worker.

Kathy shook her head. "It's new to me though."

Cynthia nodded comfortingly. "It is new to most families coming in here. Our palliative care unit is a place where we focus on helping people be as comfortable as they can while they are dealing with serious illness. Often people in palliative are no longer getting curative treatments. Instead, we want to keep the best quality of life that we can for them. And that includes having family around, if that is what they want. Can you tell me a little about your father?" she asked, looking at Mackie. Mackie turned up her hands, feeling helpless, and turned to Kathy.

"Uh, yeah," Kathy said. "He's a fisherman, and a fiddler, and he likes to play cards. He's pretty ill, Dr. Aram said, and I guess being in palliative means that we could come see him and that you would do your best to keep him out of pain, right?"

"Yes, that's right. And we set our unit up so family members can be there round the clock. You can arrange things to fit him and your family. Like his dog could come visit, if he has a dog. Or you can bring in his favorite music. If he's a fiddler, he probably likes music. Let's go take a look at the unit," Cynthia said comfortably. She led the way down the hall and to a bank of elevators. The palliative unit was on the third floor, with a lounge full of comfortable furniture, a small kitchen, a chapel, and patient rooms. Cynthia showed them around, then led them down the patient corridor and stopped outside Eric's door.

"He's just arrived here. Take some time for a visit, and then we can figure out what you need or want for the next little while," Cynthia said. "I'll check in with you a little later."

Mackie let Kathy lead the way into Eric's new room. She was barely breathing as she entered. This room reminded her of her mother's palliative room, the place where her mother died. For a moment, Mackie was transported back to Boston: city noises, hospital rushing, scary sounds. Determinedly, she refocused. That was then. This is Eric.

He was unconscious but he was breathing on his own. Mackie saw a little oxygen tube near his nose. Kathy went straight toward the bed and pulled a chair close. Leaning in, she picked up his free hand. Mackie could see Kathy's tears.

Mackie shifted uncomfortably. *I barely know this man, and I barely know Kathy*, she thought, *but here I am, sharing this intimate moment, like a real member of the family. I feel so awkward.*

She desperately wanted to get out, out of the room, out of the building, maybe even out of the country. When she closed her eyes, she relived the last time she had spoken to Eric. He had yelled at her and flipped that table at her, like a nasty, abusive old man. She could still feel the shock in her body, the fear in her belly. She knew that people said he wasn't mad anymore, but still. Mackie knew she had claimed to be determined to stay, but she felt so uncomfortable. Why on earth was she here? Eric might be her father, but Mackie could not use that as a road map. She felt lost and very much alone.

Mackie backed out of the room, heading for a chair in the communal area. She sat, heavily. Kathy was there with her dying father. Mackie felt, once again, like she had no business being here at all. She also, once she sat down, felt glued to her chair. Her determination was rising again. She was not running away. She might not be at his bedside, but she was staying in the building. Fear, loneliness, feeling lost…these were just feelings. He was her father and she was staying.

She had no idea how much time passed. She sat staring at her hands when she felt a touch on her shoulder. Declan.

"How are you doing?" He looked closely at her face.

"Oh, you know," she said. "Not great. I don't think I should even be here, but where would I be if not?" She shrugged.

He smiled ruefully and gently. He stroked her face with his palm. "This is the palliative unit, right?"

She nodded. "He's dying, Declan. He may have days when he is better, but he's dying." The words made it real. Her father, barely found, was going to die. There was a weight on Mackie's chest.

Declan nodded. "Is he awake?"

She shook her head. "No. And I don't know if he will wake up. I know from my mother that dying can take a long time. Or not so long. I just know you always wish for more time after it's over."

"Jake and the kids are going home," Declan said, "and I think I'm going to go, too. But I'll stop at your place and pick Murphy up. He can hang out with me. You might be here for a long time."

Mackie was struck with guilt. She'd barely given Murphy a thought. "Thanks so much, Declan," she murmured. "That's a big help. Poor boy, I kind of forgot about him. What time is it, anyway?"

Declan looked at the clock on the wall. "Looks like it's near seven. We've been here for a while."

"I had no idea," she said. "Time feels all out of whack."

"Yes, I can see that. Got your phone? I'll be in touch. You'll need a ride home if you decide to leave."

"Thanks, Declan. You're the best." She gave him a light hug, then gripped him and held on. "I don't know what I'd do without you," she murmured against his chest. He leaned his cheek on the top of her head.

"Don't worry about that," he said. She could hear his smile in his voice. "I'm here. Well, actually, I'm leaving to go get Murphy, but you can count on me." After a kiss on Mackie's cheek, he walked down the hall.

Kathy came out of Eric's room, eyes red-rimmed and bleary.

"What can I do, Kathy? Can I help at all?"

Kathy nodded. "Yes, you certainly can. I don't feel okay leaving Dad alone here and I also have to leave. I didn't sleep last night, and you know we were all up at four the day before. I need sleep. I also need to check in at home. I need to spend some time with Jake and my boys, make sure nobody has collapsed from sugar overload or something. Can you stay here and just text me if anything happens? I'm just beyond beat."

Mackie nodded. "Of course. I'm good. I did sleep last night. I'm happy to stay." Of course she would stay. She was the other daughter.

"Mackie, thank you. It means a lot to have you here," Kathy said, giving her an affectionate pat on the shoulder. Mackie looked after her as she trod heavily down the hallway.

Then she took a big breath and headed for Eric's room.

Mackie hesitantly stepped in the room. The midsummer sun was still strong in the early evening and the windows bright. The light illuminated Eric's pale gray face above his blanket.

She gingerly stepped to the lone chair at the bedside and perched on the edge. Here she was, next to Eric. Next to her father. Her dying father.

How could this be? How could he be dying when she just now found him?

His breathing was labored. Mackie remembered nights of listening to her mother's breathing, waiting for each next breath. She remembered the feelings overwhelming her, making her jump out of the chair and go running down the hall.

But she was here now. She was no longer that person.

Eric's breathing struggled on. Mack settled more firmly into the chair. No matter how frightening the sound, she had told Kathy she would stay, and she was determined to do that. As her body settled, she got used to the rasping sounds of Eric's breath and looked at his face. Did Kathy look like her father? Or, really, did she herself look like him? What was there in Mackie that came from Eric?

He lay still except for the breathing and that made her braver. She leaned forward and touched the back of his hand with her fingertips. Cool, very cool. She picked up his hand and held it in both of hers.

"Well, here we are," she told him, her voice small and meek. "Here we are, you and me, a father and a daughter." She looked at him carefully for any sign he could hear her. There was no movement.

"I always thought my father was a man who maybe was a hero," she breathed. "Who maybe was so busy saving the world that he didn't have time for his little girl." Eric continued to lie still, rasping breaths in and out.

"And my mother told me that. That you were too busy. And I believed her that you had more important things to do than see me. But I still wanted you to be a hero. A hero for me."

He continued to lie still.

"Then I found out she had never even told you about me. That she had wanted to ask for child support but was too afraid. That she wanted to tell you I existed, but she was scared that you'd reject her and me, too. She let me believe that you rejected me. That you wanted nothing to do with the baby you hadn't wanted.

"Now I know that she never gave you a choice. You didn't even know that you had a baby. How could you reject me if you didn't even know about me? But I didn't know any of this until a few months ago. After Mama died and I could not talk about it with her. When I had nobody left at all to care about me.

"So I thought I would come and find you, and talk with you about it. And see if, maybe, if you knew you had another daughter, that might be a beginning for us.

"Now I found out that my mother lied about a lot of things. I don't know what I can trust that she said. I know she gave me poor advice and that she was scared of living her life."

Eric lay still. Mackie looked hard at his craggy, gray face. Her words were laced with her tears now. "And now you are going to die, too. I don't want you to die! I never even got to be a daughter to you. When do I get to have a father?" Tears poured down her face now, and her quiet voice had become louder, more emphatic.

"I just wanted a family. I just wanted to know who my people are. Why is that so hard?"

She let go of Eric's hand and got up from the chair. She turned to look out the window at the early evening; long shadows, green leaves burgeoning, birds still busy in the long dusk of a Maritime summer. Her left hand fingered the medallion at her neck.

She thought about playing cribbage in the fish house, about their discussions about books, and his kind look as he dismissed her questions about cousins. She remembered his hands, carving little boats and then tipping the table, knocking her cup of coffee to the floor. She wondered what he had thought, with a grown woman showing up and claiming him as her father. What did he remember of her mother, of that summer of 1985, of the medallion hanging around Mackenzie's neck?

Mackie was aware of waves of feeling in her body; the heat of anger, the chill of fear, the jitters and nausea that came with feeling alone and guilty. She heard her mother as if she were in the room.

Kenzie, you take good care of the people you love. They're all you have in the world, so you do right by them.

Mackie turned to face Eric in the bed again. His harsh breathing was erratic. Well, she might not love him, but he was her family. She would do right by him and stay right here. And who knows if she might have learned to love him or they might have learned to love each other if they had only had more time?

She settled in to see it through.

KATHY AND MACKIE WORKED out a schedule so that someone from the family was with Eric around the clock. Between them, plus Jake and Declan and Simon, Kathy's oldest son, home from Montreal because his grandfather was dying, they took it in turns to spend nights or days at the hospital.

Kathy was on evening shift when Mackie came in to cover the night shift. Kathy had been sitting in the chair, head tipped back, possibly dozing.

"Hi," said Mackie, entering the room.

Kathy sat up, shaking her head. "Oh, time already? How you doing, Mackie?"

"Pretty good," Mackie said. "How is he?"

Kathy shrugged and the two women went to the hallway to chat. "He was restless for a while and I actually wondered if he was going to wake up," Kathy said. "But maybe it was just getting to be time for his medicine."

"Do you think he will wake up?" Mackie asked wistfully. "I have so much I want to tell him."

"You should tell him," Kathy advised. "Don't worry about him waking up. You can't predict the future. But you also don't know what he's able to hear. We don't have these conversations in there, do we? That's because we don't want him to listen in. So you might as well tell him anything you want him to know."

Mackie nodded. "Okay. Why not?"

Kathy gave her a hug. "Don't forget to get some sleep, too, sister," she said fondly. "You're there, even if you are sleeping. It counts."

"Right. Good night, Kathy."

Mackie hauled up the chair and sat next to Eric for the first half hour. There wasn't much to see. He was breathing better than a week ago since he had done some healing from the smoke inhalation. But he had not regained consciousness, though it was still possible.

She pulled out her laptop and sorted the work she planned to get done during this shift. She had neglected her business while her personal life was in upheaval, but if she planned to keep buying food, she had to get some work done.

After some time, she got up to stretch. She wandered out to the lobby to get something from the vending machine. The hospital was interesting in the middle of the night. Never really still, the building was humming. Was that from air conditioning? Something else? Even though there was a persistent hum, the overall effect was quieter than during the day.

When she went back into his room, something was different. She walked toward the bed, faint in the glow of the night light and from the hallway. Eric's eyes were open.

She rushed to his side. "Eric? Eric?"

He blinked slowly and turned his head. Mackie bent down toward him. "Hi, Eric." All the things she wanted to tell him tumbled through her mind, but she simply said, "I've missed you."

His eyes focused on her. She gave a tremulous smile. She picked up his hand and, for the first time, felt an answering pressure, however slight.

Mackie reached for her phone to call Kathy. Before she could get it out of her pocket, Eric's lips were moving. "What?" she asked. "What did you say?" She leaned her ear close to him.

"My—my girl," he whispered. Then his eyes closed again and the pressure in her hand released. He returned to the stertorous breathing he'd been doing for days.

Mackie dropped his hand and let go of her phone. *My girl? My girl.* He must have wanted Kathy. And what now? She called for the nurse to tell them that Eric had been awake and had spoken.

The nurse questioned her. "Had you been sleeping?" Mackie realized that the nurse wondered if she'd been dreaming, but Mackie had the candy bar from the vending machine to prove to herself that she'd been wide awake.

The nurse checked Eric out. "Actually, it looks like he's sleeping now. He may wake up again later."

She sent Kathy a text. There was no need to come now, as he was asleep, but there had been something. *My girl.* He wanted Kathy.

Mackie leaned back in the chair and looked at him sleeping. *He was dying, yes. But he opened his eyes, and he opened them when I was here*, she told herself with some satisfaction. *He spoke to me.* She put her feet up and closed her eyes.

"Hey! Hey, you! Mackenzie from Massachusetts, wake up." She heard the loud whisper and opened her eyes. The room was full dark, but Eric's blue eyes shone clear from the pillow. He was looking right at her. "What am I doing in this place? Did you bring the cribbage board?" Mackie watched as he rolled over and pushed himself up to sit on the edge of the bed.

He looked tiny in his hospital gown, small and hunched over. But his eyes were bright and full of fun.

"So, Miss Mackenzie, it turns out you're a Johnson after all. I wish I had known. You know, I loved your mother, at least for a summer. And I'm proud of you, proud of how you turned out. I know it took guts to come here and find me, and I know I was hard on you. Turns out you're the kind of daughter who can stay with her old man in the hospital, even when he's no fun at all." He smiled.

He seemed to sit up taller as she watched. "You're my daughter, Mackenzie, and I am proud of you. I wish I had known you as a baby, and a little girl, and even a sassy teenager. I am glad you are part of my family."

His words, spoken clearly, floated on the air between them. As she watched, fog blew into the room from the window, obscuring her view. The room was full of mist and Mackie struggled to see anything, then she struggled to sit up.

When the mist cleared, Mackie sat forward in her chair. Eric was sleeping in the bed, just as he had been. Mackie rubbed her eyes. *Now that was a dream*, she thought. *I'm not so deluded I can't tell the difference, not yet.*

Dream or not, Eric's words stayed with her. *My girl. I'm proud of you.* She felt a warmth in her chest as she thought of those words. *My girl.*

She tugged his blanket up. *My dad*, she thought. She tucked the blanket around him, kissed his forehead, and then pulled a blanket over herself in her chair. She fell asleep clutching the medallion hanging around her neck.

MACKIE TOLD DECLAN about her visitation, both the part that she was sure of and the part that was more like a dream. Declan was noncommittal but interested.

"What do you think it means?" he asked as they cleaned up after a late lunch at Mackie's house.

"I'm sure it's mostly wishful thinking on my part," Mackie answered slowly. "But maybe I am allowing myself to accept my status here. Somehow I feel more legit. Even though the last time he really saw me, he kicked me out of the building."

Declan grinned. "Just like a dad and a teenager anyway, right?"

Mackie grimaced. "It felt pretty real."

"I bet you never made your mother so mad she threw anything, right?"

Mackie had to agree. "I was a really good kid. She struggled so much, I had to be sure not to add to her struggle. She was pretty mad at me when I split up with Andrew though. I wasn't a teenager at that point."

"No, but you get my idea. Maybe you and Eric just had some, I don't know, developmental stuff to work through."

She threw a tea towel at him. "Don't talk your teacher talk to me."

But it was true. She felt different now. She felt useful to her new family. By taking the nights at the hospital, she kept Eric company and Kathy got to be home with her family. The family meetings where she and Kathy and Jake got together to discuss Eric's care were precious to her. This was unfamiliar territory.

And Declan was here. They spent most late afternoons together after Mackie had slept and he had worked on the water. Murphy was as happy to see Declan as he'd ever been to see Mackie. She was thinking of the three of them as a little unit.

"This feels a bit like the eye of the hurricane," she said to him one afternoon as they walked the beach. "Things are calm, but it's false calm, temporary. We're really waiting for Eric to die, aren't we? That's the only outcome. And it feels wrong to say this, but I really like this calm. I know we're in a crisis, but I know what my job is."

Declan nodded. "What happens after Eric dies? What will you do?"

She shrugged. "You know I have been avoiding thinking about that. I guess that's what I meant about the hurricane. When he's gone, then I have to go back into figuring things out."

He took her hand. "I've made my position clear, haven't I? Stay. Stay here. Not for me, but for you."

She snorted. "What do you mean, not for you? You don't exactly seem to be an impartial party to this conversation."

He grinned, agreeing. "I'll admit it. I want you to stay. Or I can go to Massachusetts with you, if that's where you're going."

She was shocked. "Really? You'd go away from here with me?"

"Yeah. You're not the only one who's been thinking, you know. I want to be with you for real, Mackie. Not just for this year that you've come to Stella Mare." His serious tone turned teasing. "Besides, you think you have some cachet in being 'from away,' but it turns out you're a Johnson like the other Johnsons. A local girl!"

That was Declan, making light. But he stopped and turned her toward him, holding both of her hands in his. "Sorry for making jokes. This is no joke, Mackie. I want you. I want to be with you. Stay with me, or I will go with you, but we belong together." She saw the tenderness in his eyes and felt her heart melt. She lifted her chin, and he kissed her, gently at first and then with enthusiasm. Murphy broke it up with a bark and a stick to throw. Mackie felt both shaken and deeply content.

"Yes, then. Yes, I want to be with you, too. But I still don't know what I should do next."

"Let's just decide that we'll be trying to make a joint decision, Mack. That you won't take off in the middle of the night or leave without us trying to figure things out. I'm serious about this."

She nodded. She could agree to that.

"Eric told me once that I'd think differently about this place if I had come in the winter," she said. "Maybe I won't like the winter."

Declan put his arm across her shoulders and pulled her close. "We'll figure out how to stay warm. You're not from Florida, anyway. You know what winter is like."

"I agreed to house-sit for a year. I didn't know what to expect here, but I didn't realize quite how small this town is. I thought it might take a long to time to find Eric, and to, you know, try to connect. I've never lived anywhere with so much space, so few people. I thought I could come and be incognito for months."

"Didn't work, eh?"

"Cassandra. The first person I met was Cassandra, and she pried a lot of information out of me and announced it. You were there, I think."

"Yeah, I noticed the new girl in the diner, too. I'm not quite as extroverted as Cassandra. And also not as young. But I definitely noticed you."

"I'm not complaining. Cassandra has been a good friend, and her mother, Pat, too. Plus, she got me out of a deep funk. You do know, don't you, that I might be prone to deep funks?"

"Yep," he responded comfortably. "I know you've been through a lot in the last couple of years, and you're probably entitled to your funks. You might not know about my tendencies though."

"Tendencies! You've got tendencies? You mean, like tending to be very reliable, conscientious, likes kids and dogs, and able to make a mean takeout Thai?"

"Don't idealize me, Mackie."

She laughed.

"Really." He became more serious. "I'm really just a guy trying to do his best and falling short a lot of the time."

She shook her head. "You haven't fallen short with me, Declan. You pulled Eric out of the fire. I have no idea how you found the guts to head into that building. He would have perished for sure in there."

"I had to try. I didn't know who was in there, but there was a person and I had to try. When I found out it was Eric, I was glad, because I knew you two hadn't settled anything between you."

"And we still haven't, not for real," she said, throat tightening. "Only in my dreams. It may never happen. In fact, I think it will never happen. I have to be okay with that."

"Not easy," Declan commented. "But I feel like we've settled a little between us, right?"

She nodded. Yes, they had. She would not disappear from Declan's life. He could count on her for that.

AFTER SIXTEEN DAYS of waiting and watching, Eric's death was an anticlimax. Kathy was at his side. His breathing had become more and more erratic over the last two days and it was clear that he was leaving his body. Mackie and Kathy had been in the unit more than not, spending more time together. Declan pitched in to help Jake with the boys and the farm.

Mackie had gone out to get coffee for her sister. She enjoyed thinking that. *My sister.* She asked the barista for two lattes, one decaf (*for my sister*, she said in her mind). When she got back to the room, Kathy was staring intently at Eric and there was a nurse present.

"What? What's going on?" Mackie asked.

Kathy and the nurse both waved her over. "He's going," Kathy said, eyes on Eric's face. Mackie slipped in next to Kathy, who was stroking Eric's forehead. Mackie took his hand.

"We love you, Dad," Kathy murmured. "It's okay to go. I got Mackenzie here, too. We'll be fine. We love you."

There was a long space between his breaths. After each one, Mackie wondered if that had been the last. Then she wondered about Sarah's last moments. Had it been like this? Only without her daughter to say goodbye? Tears slipped down her cheeks and she fought to stay in this moment, not to get lost in the past. Was that a breath? Or no, it was more like something else leaving his body. Over a moment Eric was no longer there. Kathy leaned in and kissed his forehead, then she turned to embrace Mackie. The two women held each other tightly, tears falling.

The nurse noted the time of death and tactfully left them.

"Well, little sister," Kathy said. "I guess that's that. Thank you for being here."

Mackie shook her head. "I appreciate you including me. I know the whole thing has been confusing and hard."

"Not hard, really. Just new. I wish Dad had more chance to get to know you. He would have been proud of who you are and I suspect he wishes he'd known a long time ago."

"That means a lot, Kathy. Thank you."

Endings and Beginnings

The entire town turned out for Eric's funeral. There was a service at the little white wooden church opposite the harbor, and Russ, Jimmy, Declan, and Jake were among the pallbearers. Kathy spoke from the pulpit.

"Many of you have known Dad longer than I have," she began. "And many of you have stories to tell. Probably most of them don't belong in church. We'll hear them over the next weeks and months. For now, though, let me say that Eric was a son of Stella Mare whose ancestors arrived here generations ago. Like his ancestors, he fished. Even after he stopped working on the water, Eric maintained the family fish house as a shrine to coffee and card games." There were smiles and nods among the congregation.

She went on, "Like his grandfather, Eric played the fiddle, always by ear, and could pick up a new tune immediately. He loved books about faraway places. His woodcarvings are displayed in the Provincial Museum. In his youth, he went to the University of Maine and developed an affection for the state that made him go back, year after year, to visit and to work.

"He was young when he went to Vietnam and he was old and broken when he returned. Not old in years, but old in spirit. He became a man of many secrets after that and would leave town for weeks on end. I lost touch with him for a while, but then later he came back into my life and I will always be grateful for that.

"Eric was a man with secrets. But there were some secrets about Eric that he didn't even know. One of them came to light early this summer. My sister, Mackenzie Brown, came to town. I didn't know I had a sister and Eric didn't know this either. But this is a gift that Eric brought to my life and I am grateful for that, too. He wasn't always a great dad, but he tried to be a good man and I will miss him every day."

Mackie sat in the front pew holding Declan's hand. She gripped it tighter with Kathy's words and felt an answering pressure from his fingers.

The informal eulogizing happened later at Jake and Kathy's house. The neighbors brought food and it seemed like everyone in town dropped by to offer condolences, raise a glass, and tell a story about Eric. Kathy's younger boys and Mackie were rapt. This was all new to them and, though Mackie thought she could separate exaggeration and good storytelling from facts, she was hard-pressed to do so. Finally she gave up trying to sort fiction from fact and just sat back to enjoy the tales.

"What about burial?" Pat asked Mackie. "Do you know what they decided?"

"Cremation," she replied. "Eric apparently asked for cremation. Kathy wants to scatter some ashes on the water later this summer."

Pat nodded. "Seems like a fitting ending. So, Mackie, you turned out to be related after all."

"Yeah. And I have a sister! Thanks so much, Pat, for helping me to decide to talk about it. I have always been so afraid of upsetting people and this really did upset people. Some secrets have to be told, though, because they might not belong only to the people who are keeping them."

Pat nodded. "That makes sense to me. All the same, I'm sure your mother had her reasons for what she did."

"She did," Mackie agreed. "I still don't know that entire story and I don't know if I ever will. I know that things must have felt overwhelming and too complicated to be fixed, so she just left. I know the feeling well."

Pat reached out to touch her hand. "I'm glad you stuck it out here, Mackie. I hope you decide to stay around."

Declan came up in time to hear her last comment. "Of course she's staying around," he said with confidence. "At least until next year."

Mackie nodded. "I told this guy that I'd be here until spring. So that's the plan, at least for now."

Pat drifted off and Mackie and Declan went out into the yard where the sun was beginning the long sink toward the horizon. They walked toward the cabin where Eric had lived his final years.

"I've never been in there, but I'm curious," Mackie admitted.

"Kathy will show you around. Probably not tonight, but sometime."

She looked at the small building, with a tiny front porch and the metal chimney that spoke of woodstove heat. She wandered up to the porch and peered in the window. Declan propped his chin on her shoulder and looked, too.

"Not much in there," he commented.

"Looks like it was just enough. A table and two chairs, a little couch, a kitchen sort of, and I guess the bedroom must be back there."

"Space for a man and his fiddle. He was at the fish house a lot and Kathy mostly fed him his meals."

"Yeah. I just wish...."

"Wish what?"

"Oh, you know. That I met him sooner. That I didn't spend my whole life imagining a father when there was a real one right here."

He drew her around to his embrace. She clung to him, feeling the heaviness of her words. "It's like I miss the father I never had now that I know I could have had him."

Declan patted her comfortingly. There wasn't much to say. After a while, she wiped her eyes. They headed back up to the house, the final car of guests heading down the driveway.

Kathy was sitting at the kitchen table with Jake. Jake had a fat envelope in his hands.

"Oh, Mackie, good, you're still here," Kathy said. "We're going to take a look at Eric's papers. His will and whatever else he had in that envelope."

Mackie sat down, fingering her medallion. Here was another place of discomfort. What did Eric's will have to do with her?

Jake flipped through a thick stack of papers. "This was written in 2009, Kathy. Was that the last time he did a will?"

She shrugged. "You knew Eric. He wasn't much of a one to talk about stuff like that. I remember that was right after his first diagnosis though. Nothing like a cancer diagnosis to make you think about your mortality."

Jake kept poking in the envelope. "Well, we've seen the 2009 will. No surprises there. But look, here's something else. Look at that, Kathy. He wrote it on the day of the beach party. That's pretty recent. The fire happened late that night, so this must be about the last thing he'd written."

Kathy peered at the card Jake held in his hand. "Geez, Dad, terrible handwriting! But let me see. This is about you, Mackie."

Mackie's heart was suddenly in her throat. "Me?" Her voice came out like a little squeak.

Declan leaned forward. "What's it say?"

Kathy read to herself and then pushed the index card across the table to Mackie and Declan. Mackie's hands were at her mouth. She shook her head. "I can't," she murmured.

"Well, I can," Declan declared and picked up the card. "'Dear Mackenzie from Massachusetts, I want you to know and everyone to know that you are my daughter. I didn't know it before and I wish I had known. Being a father was not my best thing, as Kathy can tell you, and I didn't do it any better with you. But you and Kathy are both my girls and I want that to be known. Eric K. Johnson, Stella Mare, July 13, 2017.'"

Declan looked up at Mackie. She felt herself go pale and then red, and she carefully looked at Kathy.

Kathy's eyes were kind. "I told you he got over being mad."

Mackie exhaled. "He acknowledged it. He really did. Wow. I'm not sure how I feel."

"Well, I'm sad that he's not here with us and I'm glad that you are," Kathy said clearly. "And I really wonder why he decided to put that in writing and in the envelope with his will. It's almost as if he knew that he wouldn't be around to tell you himself."

Declan and Jake looked at each other, wordless. "What was he doing down at the shore in the middle of the night anyway?" asked Mackie. "Was that usual?"

Kathy shrugged. "Well, it wasn't a usual night. For one thing, there was the beach party, and some folks were still on the beach as late as when the fire started. He probably wasn't sleeping well. He had that bad news from his doctor about his cancer, too."

"And about me," Mackie added. "I didn't pick the best day to talk to him about my mother."

Jake shook his head. "How could you know, Mackie? No point in second-guessing. He wrote this to let us know that he knew you were his kid. And so you are."

"Right. Okay, I'll take it at face value. Thank you." Mackie nodded her agreement. But it was time to change the subject. "Kathy, do you need any help cleaning up here? Declan and I are great dishwashers."

Declan grinned. "Speak for yourself, Mackie. But I can help, Kath, if you have some work to be done."

"No, we've got it. Why do you think I keep these big teenage kids around?" After hugs all around, Mackie and Declan headed out.

Epilogue

Mackie pulled into the driveway with some relief. It had been a long trip from Somerville, and she and Murphy were happy to get out of the car. In December, deep dusk arrived before five p.m. She hurried up on the porch, pulling her keys from her pocket.

The house was dark and chilly, but she turned on lamps, filled the kettle, and clicked the thermostat to heat. It wouldn't be long before it felt like home again. She could see the dog sniffing around the frosty backyard, checking to see who had been visiting recently. This place, once her home-for-now, felt like a real home. Having gone back to visit Massachusetts, she could really feel the difference. Murphy took off at a run toward the front of the house.

Before she had a chance to take off her jacket, the front door opened and the dog bounded in, followed closely by Declan. Mackie never remembered smiling so hard.

"You came back!" he crowed, swinging her around and enveloping her in a bear hug.

"Of course I did. I told you I would," she laughed. "It's only a week, you know. Come on in and have a cup of tea."

They shucked jackets and headed to the kitchen where the kettle was boiling.

"How was it? Your trip?"

She poured their tea and sat. "It was sad, I guess, and also okay. It's been a year since Mama died, as you know, and I just felt like I had some amends to make to her. I felt bad for being so angry with her since she died. I wanted to tell her how things have worked out. Standing at my mother's grave, I wished so hard that she could be here to see this, to see us, and to know about Eric and Kathy and all the ways that my life is changing. She would be happy for me. I know she would. But at the same time, I know that if she were here, if she hadn't died, I wouldn't be here. I wouldn't know about Eric, I wouldn't know Kathy, and I wouldn't even know you."

Declan looked pensive. "I can't imagine not knowing you, Mack. I would have missed out on so much. I am also sorry that I will never meet your mother."

Mackie nodded. "Me, too. I am so sorry that she had to die for me to find my roots, but I am grateful that she left me a road map to follow. I wonder so much about her. About her and Eric, and her family in Maine, and why she even wrote those letters. And maybe especially why she kept them. But I am grateful that she did. So grateful."

"Have you cleaned up some loose ends, then?"

"My mother's life still feels like a handful of loose ends. So many mysteries. But there are loose ends here, too, like Eric's will. All of that still remains to be sorted out, since he claimed me as his child. But I'm not a loose end anymore. I feel like I have found my people and my place."

"You're a Johnson from Stella Mare, even if your name is Brown. When people ask you who your people are, you'll have something to tell them."

"Yes, that's true. But Declan"—she took his hand— that isn't what I meant. It's you. You're my people and this is my place. *You* are my people. In case that wasn't clear enough for you."

She saw an unaccustomed glittering in his eyes. "So no longer Mackie from Massachusetts, right? Mackie of Stella Mare, something like that?"

"Maybe it's Mackenzie now. I once was the good little girl Kenzie. I was Kenzie to my mother and to Andrew. Kenzie was a girl who didn't know her own mind and was afraid of rejection. Then I decided I was going to be Mackie and be brave enough to search for my father. Not just someone's good little girl, but Mackie, who was strong enough to go on a quest. It was an idea, but then it became real.

"Now, though, maybe I can just be me. Not Kenzie, trying to be good, or Mackie, trying to be strong. Maybe I can be Mackenzie. Mackenzie for me, not for someone else. Or maybe..."

"Maybe Mackenzie for me, too." He stood, drawing her into his arms.

The End

Grace note with gratitude

I'm waving at all the people who have helped me write this story. Hey, you there! I'd love to get you all together for a cup of tea and talk. But since I can't, here's what I can do…. offer my thanks.

Many thanks to Lara Zielinski, editor extraordinaire, who found things in this book I didn't know I'd put here. Thanks to Claire Smith of Book Smith Designs, for her kindness and patience with a new author, and her referral to Denis Caron. Thanks to Denis, too. Without his help, you probably would never have found this book.

A deep bow to my family, who have been wonderful boosters of spirits. They include my writer daughter, Adrienne Fraser, and my superhero brother, Matthew Costello, who offered encouragement from their experiences. My thanks to my sister, Lydia Hawkins, for listening with grave interest, and to my beloved, Dan for his unending support.

I must acknowledge Max the Labrador, no longer with us, but a family member who certainly was part of the inspiration for Murphy. May your paradise be full of treats and belly scratches!

Don't miss out!

Sign up for Annie's occasional emails.

Follow the link to her website to sign up.

https://anniemballard.com/

About the Author

Annie M. Ballard loves writing, reading, baking, gardening and living in the Canadian Maritimes. A woman of uncertain age, she has been a voracious reader since age 7, when she was old enough to get her own library card. She haunted the stacks of the tiny village library where she grew up in Maine, and soaked in science fiction, poetry, literature, and humour. As a young woman, she immersed herself in cozy mysteries. She wrote her doctoral dissertation while inhaling Isaac Asimov's early stories and camping with her family up and down the east coast of the US.

Moving to the Maritimes in the early 2000s gave her access to her roots. Now, Annie writes about the lives of women and the people who love them from her home in New Brunswick, Canada. Born and raised in New England, she brings a fondness for music, baking, small-town life, and the remarkable shared ancestry of Maritimers and New Englanders to her work. Having found her own Maritime roots later in life, she seeks to make the most of her mixed heritage and embraces both "ayuh" and "eh."

To visit Annie's webpage and join her email list, click here: anniemballard.com

Made in the USA
Middletown, DE
27 September 2021